"I'm Portia Finch."

"NCIS special agent, I know." Declan couldn't help the smile.

She nodded, and a smile curled one corner of her lips. "It's nice to meet you, Declan. Despite the circumstances."

"I don't know whether to be relieved or not that the body wasn't my brother. Someone is still dead."

"I'll keep you apprised of what I find out." Portia pulled a card from the inside pocket of her coat and handed it to him.

She wasn't giving him her number for any other reason, either. Despite the first flicker of what he recognized as attraction on his part.

Just a little zing. Could be more. Was he going to find out?

"There's a whole lot of work to do to sort out this mess." Her gaze snagged on something over his shoulder. "I–"

But before she could finish, shots rang out.

Lisa Phillips is a British-born, tea-drinking, guitar-playing wife and mom of two. She and her husband lead worship together at their local church. Lisa pens high-stakes stories of mayhem and disaster where you can find made-for-each-other love that always ends in a happily-ever-after. She understands that faith is a work in progress more exciting than any story she can dream up.

Books by Lisa Phillips

Love Inspired Suspense

Secret Service Agents

Security Detail
Homefront Defenders
Yuletide Suspect
Witness in Hiding
Defense Breach
Murder Mix-Up

Double Agent
Star Witness
Manhunt
Easy Prey
Sudden Recall
Dead End

Visit the Author Profile page at Harlequin.com for more titles.

MURDER MIX-UP

LISA PHILLIPS

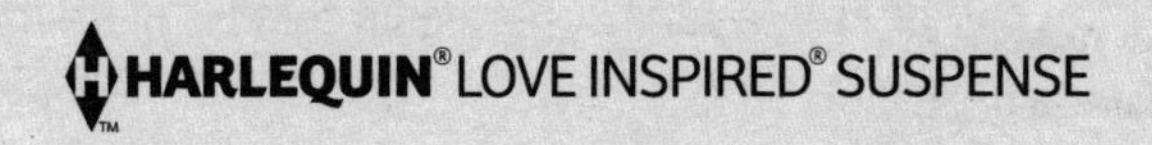

LOVE INSPIRED BOOKS

Recycling programs for this product may not exist in your area.

ISBN-13: 978-1-335-23198-7

Murder Mix-Up

This edition published by arrangement with Love Inspired Books.

www.Harlequin.com

Printed in U.S.A.

But I would strengthen you with my mouth, and the moving of my lips should asswage your grief.

—*Job* 16:5

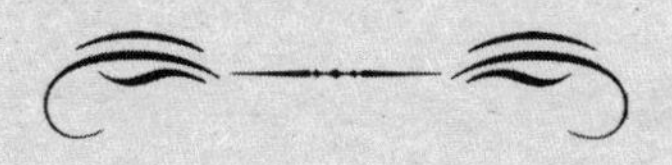

To my fabulous writer friends. Strong like Portia,
and loving like Declan. A great match!

ONE

NCIS Special Agent Portia Finch watched as the medical examiner zipped the body bag closed. Crouched as she was, her boots sinking into the soft earth of the state park, the sound eclipsed all thought for a second. Why it should hit her now—with this case, rather than all the others she'd investigated in her years as a navy cop—she didn't know.

An approaching car snapped her out of her thoughts. A silver four-door, American brand. A rental? Whoever was in the driver's seat pulled between her car, the duty SUV her teammates had driven and the medical examiner's van. Determined to be seen, whoever they were. Determined to get here.

A dark-haired man in a gray suit climbed out. Portia watched the local sheriff make his way to the man.

The medical examiner cleared his throat. He had deep lines around his wise eyes that crinkled as he stared at her with that knowing look. But he didn't ask what was in her head—not here. When he stood, his knees popped. "I'll know more about the deceased after I get him back to the office."

"Thanks, Alejandro." Portia stood while the medical examiner and his assistant lifted the body onto a stretcher.

She eyed the silver car again, then made her way over to where two of her team members were busy taking pictures of the bullet that had embedded itself in the tree.

Two gunshots, center mass. The victim, Nicholas Stringer, hadn't had time to realize what was about to happen. The fact he was a marine—the Corps being a branch of the navy—meant it was Portia's team who got to investigate.

As an agent for the Naval Criminal Investigative Service, it was her job to find the person who'd shot this young man in cold blood and left him in the middle of nowhere.

Special Agent Lenny Chen saw her approach. He gave her that chin lift guys give other guys—or their boss—instead of saying *Hi.* Older than her by a couple of years, he was a solid member of her team. Portia was honestly surprised he didn't have a team of his own yet.

She said, "About done?"

Another chin lift from Lenny.

Anna Sparrow, the other woman on the team, raised an evidence bag. The bullet was mangled, but their lab was top-notch.

"Casings?" Portia asked.

One bullet had gone straight through the victim and embedded in a tree. Alejandro had told her the second bullet was likely still lodged in the victim's chest. The more evidence they collected, the better picture they could gather of what happened. If they could find shell casings as well as the bullet…

"Got both of them," Anna said, rolling her shoulders.

"Good job." Portia glanced between them. "Both of you."

"One body, two bullets and no witnesses. The only hard part was the two-hour drive to get all the way out here in the boonies." Anna's green eyes glinted and she shook her head, her bright red hair swaying from her ponytail. "I call the backseat on the way home."

Portia heard a raised voice and glanced over her shoulder. The conversation between the suited man and the sheriff had become heated. Was the guy a reporter? He was dressed more like a fed—from one of those agencies that thought only having three letters made them better.

Portia lifted her watch. They'd been here six hours, but this wasn't a job to be rushed. Still, it was almost time to head back to the office. "Where's the kid?"

Chris Armstrong was the youngest member of their team.

"Walking the perimeter," Anna said. "Making sure we didn't miss anything." Her Boston Irish lilt was gentler now. Adrenaline brought out the fighter in her—all the fire that red hair promised. Good thing it took a lot to get her riled.

"I'll go get him." Lenny turned and wandered off.

"He's actually been kinda chatty today," Anna said.

"And his mom?"

"She had a good morning, I guess."

Lenny didn't tend to volunteer information, but he took care of his ailing mother. If she'd had a good morning that was a positive, right? Portia said, "Ready to—"

A man yelled "I want to see him!"

She whipped around. Her hand moved to her weapon as she did so, in time to see the local sheriff quickly overpowered. Just a shove, and the suited guy was past the lawman. That was when she saw it.

Silver badge.

Short dark hair, strong jaw—not that she was noticing. What was the Secret Service… Ah, the brother. Of course. Nicholas Stringer, their victim, had a brother on the president's protective detail. Evidently Declan Stringer had heard what happened and come all the way out here.

He could have identified the body at their office. And that would have been what she'd suggested when she made the call to him. Something that *hadn't happened yet*. So who called him?

Portia strode across the grass while he made his way to the stretcher Alejandro was about to load into his van. Declan Stringer tried to sidestep Alejandro, who shifted and held up one hand, matching the Secret Service agent inch-for-inch in height.

Alejandro said, "And who are you?"

The sheriff sauntered over. "This would be the deceased's brother. Declan Stringer, Secret Service."

Declan still didn't acknowledge her, or even the conversation going on around him. All his attention was on the body bag, giving her the chance to study him some more. His jaw was actually squarer up close, his hair that close-cropped, military style. Functional enough without needing gel, until it got a little longer and required taming.

He was handsome, probably a little older than her, maybe late thirties. He stood with a bearing that said he knew exactly who he was—and what he was capable of. A professional. One of those *Don't worry, ma'am. I've got this* type of guys. She'd seen a hundred of them in her line of work. And she'd had to prove to each of them that despite the colossal horror of her being *female*, she was in fact perfectly capable of doing her job.

"Agent Stringer, if you'll step aside with me. I'd like to speak with you."

"I want to see my brother." He was still facing down Alejandro.

The medical examiner glanced at her.

Portia would rather talk to Stringer first, get him to do this back at the office, but Stringer wasn't going to back down. She nodded once, then turned to the sheriff and waved him two steps away. Might as well ask the sheriff a question or two while Declan Stringer identified his brother.

She moved half a dozen steps assuming the sheriff would follow, then turned and squared her shoulders. His attention was half on her, half on the Secret Service guy. "Want to tell me why the next of kin is here?"

No remorse showed on the older man's face as he glanced at her, despite the fact he had zero jurisdiction in this case. And he certainly shouldn't have been calling the family. But this guy had been the duly elected sheriff of this county for forty-two years. By now there was no other way to do things. Just *his*.

Reminded Portia of her father.

The sheriff said, "When I saw the ID, I ran his name. Marine, brother in high places. Figured I'd help y'all out, get the word across the wires. Called you. Called the Secret Service."

And Declan Stringer had hopped the first plane from DC as early as when the call had gone out to her and the rest of her team at the Northwest Field Office. Portia sighed. It was time for them to get the body to the morgue.

"I don't hear a thanks."

She sent the sheriff a look that was probably overkill, but he seemed not to understand subtle. Then she wandered over to where the Secret Service agent stood. Back straight, his face completely impassive. She didn't want to think about how hard this was for him. If she did that—if she empathized—she would end up personalizing this case. She'd start to *feel* everything, which would kill her objectivity. Not a good plan. Especially when they saw the worst people could do to each other as frequently as they did.

Alejandro had pulled back the zipper, revealing the face of their dead marine. Nicholas Stringer's file said he worked out of the same navy base where their office was. So what was he doing all the way out here in the wild? Alejandro's liver temp calculation had put the approximate time of death at between ten last night, and midnight. Nicholas had lain on the grass all night before an early-morning hiker had found him.

The guy wasn't dressed for exercise. Boots, jeans, sweater and jacket. It was cold enough that Portia was wearing gloves. What had Nicholas been doing out here? Surely not hiking.

Alejandro said, "If you could—"

"Thank you, I've seen enough."

The voice halted her steps. Deep. Full of authority, and a sadness that made her want to hug him. Was he the brooding type? Portia needed to get the guy through this, and then get herself back to closing the case. She didn't need her resolve tested, no matter how tempting the idea of a handsome man might be. Relationships didn't work, not when you dug below the attractive exterior and actually tried to build something real. Love never lasted. What was the point of proving—again—that she was right?

"This isn't my brother."

"Excuse me?" The medical examiner had a soft tone. Kind. Or at least he had the presence of mind enough to understand the circumstances. But it wasn't necessary for them to treat Declan like he was the relative of this deceased man.

He wanted to hang his head in relief. Just bend forward, stick his hands on his knees and take a few deep breaths. It wasn't Nicholas. This was all just a day wasted. A mistake. But instead of broadcasting his relief to these people he didn't know, Declan glanced at each of them.

The sheriff. The NCIS agent. The medical examiner. "This isn't my brother." And he'd flown all the way from DC to be the one to tell them this.

But if he had to be honest with himself, he'd needed it.

Plane flights—the emotional stress notwithstanding. The waiting. Sitting. Walking. He'd been rapidly approaching burnout when he got that call. Coming off a long night of little activity on the White House grounds. The break had been good, even if it had been about trying to sleep while traveling across the country to identify his brother's body.

Declan turned to face down the sheriff. "You said Nicholas Stringer. Right? That is what you said." The sheriff gave him nothing. "Want to explain why you gave my brother's name, when this is not my brother?"

"Driver's license," the sheriff stated. No inflection, no sign of an apology. "Credit cards. All there in his wallet."

So someone had stolen Nicholas's identity? Surely they could spot a fake ID. The NCIS woman who seemed to be in charge continued her study of him. He'd been aware of her stare for a couple of minutes now. Assessing him? Maybe. Did she consider him a suspect?

If she wasn't going to apologize for this mistake, that was fine. Declan could deal. "Someone want to tell me how it's possible you falsely ID'd this man?" He hadn't seen Nicholas in a few years...was it four already? How could that be? Still, he hadn't forgotten what his brother looked like.

"Driver's license," the sheriff said. "Credit cards."

Like Declan was dense, or something.

The NCIS agent-in-charge turned to the sheriff then. "Want to tell me again how you were being helpful?"

Three other agents had drawn up around them. Ball caps, with NCIS on the front. Office attire and rain jackets, badges and guns. All of them had protective stances. They'd go to battle for this woman, their boss. And the local sheriff ranked about as high in their estimation as a stinkbug.

Declan looked at the dead body again. Relief swept through him once more, quickly followed by that grief. Someone had died. It just hadn't been his brother. The sorrow he'd nursed since that phone call early this morning was still there.

I'm sorry for your loss had to be said. But to who? The next of kin wasn't here. It was supposed to be him.

He caught her dark-brown gaze. Her hair hung past her shoulders, layered curls in different shades of brown. Her clothes were professional, but not so stuffy-looking that she didn't seem completely at home out here in the mountains. The woman was an enigma for sure—and he hadn't been that curious about a woman for a long time. Not that he allowed himself to dwell on it long enough to do more than register the feeling. She was not a mystery he planned on solving.

Declan's head was too full of work. Being a Secret Service agent on the president's detail was taxing to the extreme. A killer schedule. Long days. He didn't know how the man kept going for that long, and it pushed them all to keep up with him. Considering they were the best of the best of federal agents, that only made him respect the president all the more.

She said, "I apologize for the fact you had to come all the way out here."

Declan nodded. "Thank you." And he was sincere. He really did appreciate her apology.

The medical examiner and his assistant pushed the stretcher to their van, and the sheriff followed along behind. Which left Declan with the four NCIS agents.

The woman in charge glanced at her team. "You guys head back. I'll follow shortly."

The redhead and the younger man started walking in the direction of the vehicles. The third NCIS agent teammate said, "Boss?"

"I'm good, Lenny."

Declan could appreciate the guy not wanting to leave a woman alone with an unknown man. She was also this Lenny's boss, so he respected her answer. But the look he shot Declan spoke clearly that he didn't like the idea.

"Like I said—" She shot him a professional smile. "—I'm sorry you got dragged all the way across the country."

Declan shrugged. "We might not be super close, but he's family."

"And now we've wasted your time."

Maybe not. "I have a few days off. I'd like to know who this man was, carrying my brother's ID."

"He probably had it made recently, considering the photo is of our victim but the name is your brother's." She pulled her phone out. "You have a contact number for him?"

"I…usually just email him." He gave her the address, and she typed it into her phone.

"We'll figure it out."

He stuck his hand out. "I'm Declan Stringer."

"Secret Service, I know. Again, I'm sorry the sheriff wasted your time." She put her hand in his and they shook, his cold hand to her wool glove. "I'm Portia Finch."

"NCIS Special Agent, I know." He couldn't help the smile. "And thank you for apologizing, I really do appreciate it."

She nodded, and a smile curled one corner of her lips. "It's nice to meet you, Declan. Despite the circumstances."

"I don't know whether to be relieved or not. I mean, I am, but someone is still dead."

"I'll keep you apprised of what I find out." Portia pulled a card from the inside pocket of her coat and handed it to him. Office number. Email address. Cell phone.

He'd rather stick around and see what they learned than be filled in later. "Thanks." He managed to get the word out, even while he decided it was just professional courtesy.

She wasn't giving him her number for any other reason, either. Despite the first flicker of what he recognized as attraction on his part.

Just a little zing. Could be more. Was he going to find out? No. Declan didn't need the added complication of a relationship when he was facing some unsettling feelings about the toll his job was taking on him. He had four days off, and a decision to make. One that had to be all about him and what he wanted for the future. It didn't need to be about a cute brunette with serious eyes, who was just doing her job.

The medical examiner's van pulled away, followed by the sheriff's Jeep. Her teammates took a little longer, idling for a minute in their car before they trailed after the others. That left his rental and her car.

"Time to head out?"

Portia Finch nodded. "Two-hour drive back to the office, then a whole lot of work to do to sort out this mess." Her gaze snagged on something over his shoulder. "I—"

Before he could ask her what it was, shots rang out.

TWO

A bullet smacked the tree beside her. Portia ducked and rushed to another tree for cover, whispering a prayer for protection. Where that inclination came from, she didn't know. And now wasn't the time to figure out why she was praying after so long.

She scanned the area and searched for the shooter. Declan had found a tree ten feet from her and huddled behind it, his gun held in a loose aim. Ready. She could appreciate a competent man she didn't have to coddle.

The next shot hit the tree beside him.

Not good, but it gave her an approximate location for the shooter. Portia raced toward the origin, moving in an arc that would put her on his right flank. Another shot rang out in Declan's direction and she heard him return fire.

She caught sight of their assailant then. Dark blue jacket. Ball cap. Caucasian. Forties, maybe. She couldn't get a good enough look at his face.

"Drop the gun!"

He swung it toward her.

Portia fired, then dived. Forced to hit the ground as the shooter did the same. She heard his muffled cry of pained alarm, then footsteps cracking branches and shifting leaves. She'd hit him.

"Portia!" Declan raced toward her while the shooter got away. "Are you okay?"

"I'm fine. Go get him!" Nothing bruised but her ego, she stood and brushed leaves from her behind while she ran after him.

An engine fired up, and what sounded like a diesel truck roared away.

"He got away."

Like she couldn't see that for herself? "I don't suppose you managed to see a license plate?"

Declan shook his head. "Tan truck. Chevy."

"Older model, diesel."

His eyebrows lifted.

Portia shrugged one shoulder and headed for her car. "It chugged a little before the engine turned over. Could just be cold, but more likely he has a clogged fuel filter."

Silence. "He was holding his shoulder. I think you hit him."

She nodded. Listened to his footsteps bringing up the rear. Shame this wasn't a leisurely hike through the park. Not that she did anything in a leisurely way, but she enjoyed recreation. So long as no one pestered her with comments or questions, she could get along quite nicely with whoever accompanied her.

And yes, she realized that at thirty-four she likely shouldn't be quite this set in her ways. But she was who she was: the daughter of a marine gunnery sergeant and single father who not only taught her how to shoot but also taught her everything he knew about cars. Tears were unacceptable, unless they were angry tears—in which case she'd been sent to the garage to work out her frustration on the heavy bag.

She was also the youngest female senior field agent NCIS had. Declan might be a hotshot Secret Service agent, but she'd fought every day to garner the respect she'd earned along with her seniority.

She stared him down over her shoulder. "You'll need to come in to the office and give a statement."

"I can do that." His footsteps sped up until he walked alongside her. "Why do you seem super calm, and not like you just got in a gunfight?"

She put her weapon away. Was it just adrenaline, or was this man the most cooperative witness ever? "The shooter got away."

Declan shook his head. "That was fast. Like, seconds and it was over." He blew out a breath. "Things don't happen that quickly at the White House. We see it coming, and we respond in the applicable way. Then we do hours of paperwork while the person is processed and interviewed, then sent to jail."

"In that case, about the only similarity between our jobs is the paperwork." She shot him a look, and he smiled.

"Why does that not surprise me?" He paused. "Are we going to inform the sheriff of what just happened?"

"We are on his turf. But until I know that wasn't related to my case, there's no need. It's my investigation." And that guy had stuck around purely for the chance to shoot at a second person. Declan. "Not at me."

"What was that?"

"He wasn't shooting at me." Portia slowed beside his rental car and said, "He wasn't even interested in me until I called him out. That man wanted *you* dead."

"You think he's the one who shot my...your victim."

"Could be he thought that was your brother and he killed him. He might have it in for both of you." And why would that be? "Anyone you know who might want to hurt the two of you?"

Declan swallowed.

Portia waited.

"I'd like to hold off on story time until I know it's necessary for me to tell you."

She folded her arms. "It's necessary."

He didn't back down. "Still. I'd like to maintain my privacy until I know it's related to your case."

Sure, throw her words back at her. Portia said, "That won't fly for long."

"Just until I know for sure."

An uncooperative witness was the last thing she needed. Portia turned to her car, then said over her shoulder, "I expect you at the office, giving your statement on the shooting that just occurred, as well as your description of the truck. Soon as you get there."

She'd get the rest of the story out of him then. As well as have her people dig into Declan Stringer's background to find out everything there was to know.

"I'll check into a hotel and come straight over."

"Fair enough." She could accept the fact he wasn't a man to be pushed around, even if it made her life a little harder that he wasn't…malleable. Portia was way too type A to respect a man she could manipulate. "I'll see you there."

She had to walk away. It was that or stare into those dark eyes some more…and probably forget she had work to get on with. Attraction was one thing—she just had to get done what she needed to in spite of it—but a relationship was a whole different animal. One she wasn't ever going to go near again, considering the last one had been a disaster.

Her dad had never gotten over her mom leaving the way she had. One day there, the next, stuff gone. Suitcase gone. Car gone. They'd never seen her again.

Probably Portia hadn't ever gotten over it either. She figured that was true even if she had no intention of ever discussing it with a professional. Too much work to do to see the shrink. And as excuses went, it was the best she'd ever come up with. Get up, go to work. What free time she had, Portia tested her limits rock climbing, bouldering. Strength was more than just physical, it was also mental. And she could see it in Declan Stringer.

Too bad there was intentionally no room left in her life for a relationship—even if she was looking for one. Which she was not. It was just easier that way.

Portia turned up the talk radio station loud enough for it to drown out her whirling thoughts and gripped the steering wheel as she drove. Watching for that tan truck all the way back to Seattle.

Declan was wrong. The gunfight had affected her. It was just that it took longer than a couple of minutes. She shifted in the seat. Process the fear, set it aside. Not something she was about to do in front of anyone. She wasn't without weaknesses; she just didn't acknowledge them. Just like her father had taught her.

It was almost six in the evening by the time she got back to the office, but everyone was there. Portia set her weapon in the top drawer of her desk and said "Who wants to go first?"

Lenny, Anna and Chris just looked at each other. No one spoke.

"One of you must have *something* to explain how our dead man has his picture on a marine's ID."

Anna winced, then motioned to the director's office with a nod of her head. Portia glanced over and saw her boss, Director Elenor Golden, shake Declan's hand.

Portia was mad. Declan could tell as much as he trailed after the director. Portia glanced between her boss and Declan, shooting him a look he couldn't confuse. Yes, he'd gone straight over her head to speak with her boss. But he had a good reason.

He really wanted to know how the dead guy had been found with his brother's ID—and why the man had been killed.

He needed to know if there was a threat to his family.

After all these years?

The idea had niggled at him for the first hour of drive time before he'd made a few phone calls. Now he wanted to know badly enough to have used his not inconsiderable pull to get on this case. Not working it. Just close enough that he could observe.

What else was he going to do with his vacation?

"Special Agent Finch."

Portia stood, and her boss explained exactly what they'd just discussed in her office. The director had a strong presence, but the person in the room who arrested him…made him want to stutter…was Portia.

Her gaze came to him, a frown on her face.

"Run down the case." The director stepped to the side, and turned toward her office. "And figure this out."

"Yes, ma'am." Portia's voice was cold. There was no other way to describe it. She looked at him with a *What did you do*? face.

"Guess I'm sticking around for a while." If it took longer than four days, he'd have to call his own director and work something out.

Portia spun on her heel and strode back to her desk. The woman was a consummate professional, but there was no way she was going to simply roll over and invite him into her fold. And judging by the looks on the other agent's faces, the rest of them weren't going to give him anything either.

"Okay, run down what we—" Her phone rang. She

snapped up the receiver. "Finch." She listened for a second. Her gaze darted to him and he thought he saw a gleam of something flash there, but it disappeared just as fast. "Great. *We'll* be right there." She hung up.

"Alejandro wants us in the morgue." She strode past the desks of her colleagues and didn't even look at him. "You're with me, Stringer."

Declan followed her to the elevator, where Portia jabbed at the button for the basement a little harder than was probably necessary. He sighed. "Look—"

She cut him off. "Don't. You made your play and now we have to live with it. So let me get on with this case, and then you can be on your way."

Yep, she didn't feel the attraction. If she did, there was no way she'd dismiss him like this. Not that he wanted warm and fuzzy between them. Declan was interested in one thing—finding out what this murder had to do with his brother. Anything that could've been between him and Portia, he didn't want it clogging up getting to the bottom of this mystery anyway. The fact she felt nothing for him was a bonus.

"If there's one thing I can't abide, it's liars."

Declan bristled. "When did I—"

"You said you were going to check into your hotel. Not that you were going to come straight here. I'm surprised you didn't get a speeding ticket for how fast you had to be driving to get here ahead of me *and* get in a meeting with the director. All just so you could weasel your way into my case."

"I checked in online."

"While you were driving?"

"Quick rest-stop break," he said. "You didn't need to stop?"

"It's a two-hour drive. I'm not five years old."

Ouch. "Look, I'm sorry—"

"No, you're not. And don't patronize me by pretending to be. You wanted in, so you got yourself in." The elevator doors slid open.

"I was going to say sorry about going behind your back, but my way was faster." He was results oriented. It was the way he was trained. After all, if he misstepped by taking too long to make a decision, it could cost the president his life.

"That doesn't mean I have to like it."

She knocked twice on the door. A buzzer sounded, and Portia let herself into the morgue. Alejandro looked up, saw Declan behind her. His perfect eyebrows rose. Even with some kind of goopy mess on his gloves, the man didn't have a hair out of place. He switched the gloves out for clean ones, and Declan got his first look at the beginning of an autopsy.

"Company?"

Portia said, "He's shadowing the case."

Alejandro eyed Declan, then said, "Two gunshot wounds, one through and through and one in the sternum."

She folded her arms. "We already knew that."

Alejandro glanced at Portia.

"Sorry."

He shook his head, all forgiven. Then said to Declan, "I can get you a mask if the smell…"

It wasn't bad, per se. The room was ventilated. Still, the smell was interesting. Declan saw the curl in the corner of Portia's lips.

This was why she'd jumped at the chance to bring him down here. She thought she could get him in front of a dead body and he'd lose his lunch? He nearly smiled at the realization. The NCIS agent was testing his mettle.

Forcing him to walk in her shoes and deal with what she saw every day.

He probably should have been insulted by that. But meeting a woman who held her own, who expected a man to not cower but meet the challenge? There was nothing more attractive than strength like that. A woman who knew what she wanted and didn't settle for anything less.

Declan had to push aside the rush of thought. He wanted to go over all that, to process this revelation and set it aside so he could focus, but there wasn't even time to do that. They were waiting.

He lifted his chin instead, and turned to the medical examiner. "So the victim probably knew the shooter?"

Alejandro said, "From the velocity of impact, and the damage it did—which I'll have to confirm after I'm done with the full autopsy—I'd say at this point that it was three feet, maximum."

Portia said, "Only someone you know, and trust, or someone you're doing a deal with, gets that close. Unless the shooter was fast enough to pull off two shots." She shrugged. "But if the shots were straight on then they were facing each other."

She backed up three feet and held her arms up in front, making a gun with her fingers and holding it in her other palm.

"So they were talking, and the shooter pulled out a gun," Declan said. "Fast enough the man didn't turn away to run."

She nodded.

Alejandro said, "I'll let you know if I learn more."

Portia thanked the medical examiner, and they headed for the hallway.

In the elevator, Declan said, "I can't imagine not reacting at all if someone pulled a gun on me."

"They were probably talking," Portia said. "One second, conversation. The next he's got his gun up and he's firing two shots. Caught the guy off guard, close enough to make sure he absolutely got the job done. And then he stuck around to shoot at you hours later."

She squared her shoulders in a way that didn't bode well. "Want to tell me *now* who has it in for you and your brother badly enough to go to all this trouble?"

"You're assuming the killer is the same person who shot at us." He paused. "We don't know that."

"You'd rather there were two gunmen?"

The doors slid open and Declan exited the elevator. Maybe if there were, she could find her suspect.

And he'd never have to tell her the truth about his.

THREE

Portia sat at her desk while Declan hovered at the big TV screen, staring at the open tabs of all the information they'd collected so far. What was he hiding? And why couldn't he just tell her? Whatever it was, she figured it was wrapped up in the reason his brother had been a target.

Assuming that was what had happened.

The fact their dead guy had been using Nicholas Stringer's ID might simply be a coincidence. Then again, considering Declan was acting this way at all, likely not. There was a reason they were seemingly targets of a murderer. And he knew what that reason was.

She let him have his silence while she answered a few emails. Distracting herself from all the questions. When she was done, she moved to stand by him. "Well?"

"I should speak with my brother first."

Portia saw the flinch in the skin around Declan's eyes. He'd hidden his discomfort well, and she was getting the idea he would endure a lot before he broke that professional demeanor. Yes, bringing him down to autopsy had been a test. But if the guy was going to insinuate himself into her murder investigation then he was going to have to be all in with every part. It was what he'd asked for.

"I'll contact your brother's Captain and get him online for a chat with you."

Nicholas Stringer—the real one, not the man their victim had pretended to be. Declan's brother's Marine unit was based out of Camp Pendleton in California—not here in Washington State where the ID had indicated. Which made her wonder why that was what had come up when they entered his name into their system. This was a more elaborate identity theft than she was used to seeing.

She said, "The system says your brother is deployed right now. He's been in J-bad for nine months."

Declan frowned. "J-bad?"

"Jalalabad, Afghanistan. There's a forward operating base there." She saw the look on Declan's face. "You didn't know he was deployed."

He shrugged. "We aren't that close."

"I don't have any siblings, so I wouldn't even know how that works."

"No?"

Portia shook her head. "It was just me and my dad."

Empathy shone in his eyes. He said, "It's been just me and Nicholas for years, though we have some extended family. He and I should probably talk more, but once you get in the habit of not picking up the phone it's hard to change things." He stretched his arms up over his head, then twisted left and right. "How about you and your dad?"

"He passed away two years ago." The words were choked.

Portia didn't wait for Declan to offer her condolences. She needed to focus on the case anyway, the way she'd been keeping her attention on her job since her dad had passed. What was the point in expending the energy to grieve, letting all the feeling swallow her whole, if it wasn't going to change anything?

"Agent Armstrong," she called out to Chris as she walked back to her desk. "Get me Corporal Stringer on-screen in MTAC." It was probably about breakfast time in Afghanistan.

Their Multiple Threat Alert Center was a twin to the one at the Quantico office of NCIS. It was basically just a fancy name for a room where they gathered intelligence and could make secure communications.

"Sure thing, boss." The kid's Southern drawl sounded almost sarcastic. She eyed the probationary agent, and he shot her a grin. She sighed. Did he take anything seriously?

Lenny sat at his desk, across from Chris, frowning at his colleague.

Portia wandered over. "It's late." She spoke to Lenny in a low tone. "If you want to take off, we can hold down the fort. Catch you up in the morning."

She could likely use his help, but Lenny needed to be home as much as possible. Working this case late into the night might help with the time zone in Afghanistan, but it wouldn't help Lenny make sure his mother got to bed.

Lenny gathered his things and said good-night. Anna wandered over and clicked the remote that worked the TV screen between Chris's and Lenny's desks. "Update?"

Portia nodded. "Please."

"I dug into the military record for Corporal Nicholas Stringer," Anna said.

Portia held her hand up. "The driver's license ID for the marine based in Washington, or the real one for Declan's brother out of California?"

"Both."

"Okay," Portia said.

"As for the real Nicholas, there isn't much but standard stuff. I found some interesting things on the Washington one I punted to Squire."

Declan took a step closer to them. "Squire?"

Portia glanced at him. "Our forensic technician."

Anna continued, "Squire has the bullet, the shell casings and the deceased's clothes, so it might take a while, but I'm having him look into a lease. Someone is renting an apartment in Tacoma under the name Nicholas Stringer. I think our dead guy had his ID for a few weeks, at least. Long enough to make a life here."

Portia nodded. "Social media?"

Anna said, "I had the same thought. I ran his photo in an online search and got a hit that indicates this is bigger than one fabricated ID. A single social media profile with the deceased's picture and the name Nicholas Stringer. A couple of video shares was all he posted."

Portia felt her eyebrows rise. "It's a dummy account?"

"Set up two months ago. Before that, no digital footprint."

"Some presence is less suspicious than no presence at all."

Declan said, "What does that mean?"

Portia pointed to the profile Anna had put on-screen. "Someone who wants to stay hidden can stay off the internet, right? Just don't sign up for those accounts and you're anonymous. But it's so uncommon these days that it's actually kind of suspicious."

"Because most people have social media accounts now."

Portia nodded. "So they create a dummy profile. Just enough activity it gets a search result, but doesn't give anything personal away. He wanted to be seen online using Nicholas Stringer's ID."

"How about you?" Declan lifted his chin. "Are you on these sites?"

"Most cops have a fake profile."

"That doesn't answer my question."

This time it was Portia who lifted her chin. "Then I guess we're even."

Anna cleared her throat. "Uh…okay. So I'm going back to my desk now."

Portia glanced at the agent and caught her smiling as she walked away. Declan opened his mouth to say something, but was cut off when Chris called down from the top of the stairs at the far end of the room.

"Stringer. Your brother will be on the line in T-minus two minutes."

Declan headed for the stairs. Portia followed, and at the bottom step he turned to her. "Are you planning to listen in on my call?"

"I'll give you privacy if you need it, but I also have questions for your brother that are pertinent to this investigation."

He looked at her like he didn't know if he believed her. Whether he did or not, she was about to get an answer to her question. One way or another she would find out what Declan was hiding.

"It's routine," she assured him. "And while your brother is at least safe from a murderer over in Afghanistan, I need to know whether you'll continue to be in danger here."

Declan shook his head and climbed the stairs. "He's safe in the line of fire, and I'm the one in danger?"

"We can protect you."

"It's usually me standing between the gun and the president, doing the protecting."

"With a team of people, all currently occupied with that job. So you let us do *this* for you."

He stood with his hand on the door handle of the secure room. “And if I don’t need you to do that for me? What if I can protect myself perfectly well?”

“Never hurts to have help.”

He went inside. Portia winced, realizing she actually agreed with him. She would go it alone and take care of herself every single time. Maybe she and Declan Stringer were more alike than she’d thought.

They were nothing alike. The thought stuck with him while he donned the headphones and sat at a desk in their secure room. The video chat loaded on-screen.

Declan didn’t make a move without the backup of other Secret Service agents. Yes, he believed he could protect himself alone. But only because his instinct was to return to his team and that safety net.

Could he really do that?

If he brought danger back to the White House, he’d be putting lives in jeopardy. As a Secret Service agent, he couldn’t do that. If hc was going to maintain operational security on duty this needed to be cleared up before he went back to DC.

The screen flickered and Nicholas’s face was there. Not happy. “What’s up?”

“Hey, Nick.” Declan’s throat closed. He cleared it. “Good to see you. It’s been a long time.” The awkwardness was compounded by the fact Portia was listening to everything.

“There a reason why I hit my bunk for half an hour and then got woken up to exchange small talk with you?”

Apparently not much had changed. Nicholas was still mad about the fact their family’s history had been tarnished. And despite it being no fault of Declan’s—the two of them had been kids when their father broke the law—Nicholas still unloaded all his frustration on his sibling. Declan.

"Night duty?"

Nicholas didn't give him anything.

Declan sighed, then explained all that had happened with the dead guy.

Nicholas's eyebrows lifted. "He lives up there, by Seattle?"

Declan nodded. "Someone rented an apartment in Tacoma. He listed his occupation as 'marine.'"

"But I'm based out of Camp Pendleton. Southern California."

"I know." Declan smiled. He was pleased for his brother, even not knowing much about his life. It shouldn't be a surprise—not a good one anyway—learning something so simple. "And a Corporal now?"

Nicholas didn't reply. "Is there anything else?"

It was Portia who said, "You have an idea why a man is using your identity?" She'd leaned down close enough a strand of her hair tickled the side of his face. "He has a driver's license and credit cards."

Nicholas's gaze shifted to her, and Declan saw something there. What he didn't know was whether it was about Portia or the question.

Nicholas said, "I'm in Afghanistan. How do I know what's happening in Washington State? I can tell you my wallet was stolen a few months back. Happened to a couple of other guys in my squad, as well. I canceled my cards and got a new driver's license." He shrugged.

"Fair enough," Portia said. "But the question had to be asked."

"Can I get back to sleep now?"

"I need to talk to you about something first," Declan said. "The man who killed this guy with your ID, he waited around—or came back—and shot at me. Special Agent Finch thinks someone might have it in for us." He let that settle in with his brother, then said, "I'm going to fill her in on our…history."

"Not my history."

"I know you want to bury your head in the sand, but that doesn't mean you've moved on." At least, that was the way his shrink had explained it. "You're still mad. Apparently, at me. And while it is in the past, it's also part of us."

Nicholas leaned back in his chair. It was written all over his face that he didn't want to hear what Declan said.

He was going to say it anyway. "I want you to be careful."

"I'm in a war zone."

"You know what I mean, Nick. I don't think this guy is going to come after you there, but he shot at me. He's committed enough he found someone with your name, met with him and shot him dead." Declan blew out a breath. "That guy is dead because of us."

"Not my fault."

"That's not what I meant." Declan ground his back teeth for a second. "I just want you to be aware, so you can be safe."

"I'll be careful. Now, are we done?"

He sighed. Nodded.

Nicholas clicked off the call, halfway out of his chair before the screen blanked.

Declan leaned back and blew out a breath. When he glanced up at Portia she had a compassionate look on her face. He almost told her right then.

"Coffee?"

Declan looked at his watch. Nine thirty-four in the evening. "I doubt I'll sleep a wink, so sure."

She took him to a break room. When she placed the

mug in front of him and sat, he didn't waste any time. "My real name isn't Declan Stringer. It's Declan Harris. My brother and I changed our names when we moved in with our aunt and uncle. We didn't want to be those kids, the ones whose father had swindled investors out of millions and stashed it all in an offshore account."

She didn't sip her coffee. Portia just watched him, and fingered the handle of her mug. Listened.

"He was caught. Tried. The whole thing was a Ponzi scheme. When he went to prison we were left with nothing."

Nothing but each other and their aunt and uncle, and even that had turned sour. Declan and his brother hadn't ever been best friends, the way brothers could be. They were too different. Nicholas internalized everything, and he never let a single thing go. Declan couldn't live with that kind of bitterness. He'd had to figure out how to work the feeling out.

He said, "Dad got out of prison six years ago. Nicholas had just graduated from high school. Dad called, said he wanted to see us both. Only I showed up. My brother wasn't interested. Dad never came, though. I never saw him again."

Portia's jaw clenched, and he recalled how she'd told him her own father had died.

He said, "I'm sorry if this brings up bad memories."

"You're worried about me?" She waved away his concern, her coffee mug still untouched. "Don't be. I'm fine."

Declan wasn't convinced that was true.

"I'll look into the people your father swindled. See if there's anyone who might still be around to want revenge. People like that usually aren't quiet about their intentions."

She asked him about the tan truck the assailant had

driven away in, and he told her everything he remembered. They compiled a description together, and she had him write it all down. Sign it.

At the end she said, “It’s not much to go on. Not even really enough for a BOLO, since we don’t have a sketch of the man. The sheriff can keep his eye out for a tan truck and a Caucasian man in his forties. Dark clothes, with a ball cap. But there’s no way to narrow that down.”

He thought over everything. “You really think I’m still in danger?”

“Don’t drop your guard. Not until we figure out who your father wronged. Whoever it is could be the one who wants you and your brother dead.”

He opened his mouth to tell her he’d be careful and wound up doing a jaw-popping yawn. “I should probably get some rest.” Things would make more sense in the morning. He’d be able to make a plan. See what else these NCIS agents had come up with. Maybe they’d even find the guy tomorrow. “You don’t think it’s his real identity that got him killed. So it must be some other reason than my brother’s name as well?”

“I’m not ruling out either of those theories. We’re trying to figure out who the deceased really is, running his prints and such.” She got up. “But we’re also not going to assume you aren’t in danger. Until we know for sure, we *can’t* make assumptions.”

Declan nodded. That made sense.

Especially halfway to the hotel, when he realized he was being followed.

By a tan truck.

FOUR

It wasn't far to the hotel, but Portia kept her car behind Declan's on Charleston Boulevard. Close enough to keep him in sight, but not so close he'd see her. There was no way she was going to let even a trained Secret Service agent go it alone when there was a gunman loose. If Declan figured out she was behind him—doubtful, since she was trained at this—she would simply tell him it was about the case.

Her dead guy. Her killer. Her arrest to make.

He'd probably feel better thinking she'd essentially made him the bait by following him, half expecting that same truck to show up. But it would be worse if he thought she was trying to protect him. She wouldn't admit it was a little bit of both—along with a side of keeping her eye on a man who'd insinuated himself into her work life. It didn't matter what his reasoning was, he'd gone behind her back to get on the case.

Portia intended to nurse the sting of that rather than think about the attraction she felt between them every time he turned those dark eyes to her. Soon enough he was going to hop a plane back to his White House detail and she would probably never see him again. There was zero point in even considering anything more than a professional détente.

And yes, that was probably mostly about self-preservation. Not because of what he'd told her about his father. It would be unfair to consider him guilty for something that had nothing to do with him. It wasn't anything he'd been able to change about his life—who his father was, and what he'd done. She'd seen enough pain on his face to know he'd come through it and found at least a measure of peace on the other side. He wasn't harboring anger still. Not like his brother.

Portia changed lanes, pushing aside those thoughts. She wasn't the one who would heal what was wrong with either of them. Their family was none of her business.

A tan truck edged up on her left. Portia glanced aside, then back at the road in front of her. Declan's car was four in front of hers. She held her place in the middle lane while the truck pressed on. Until it was only red lights in front of her. No rear license plate that she'd seen.

She edged closer, shortening the gap between them so she could make sure. So she could be close if, or when, the shooter made a move.

Declan tapped his brakes. Had he seen the truck in his rearview? Maybe he'd even spotted it before she did.

Portia bit her lip and glanced at the center display. The truck driver hadn't done anything yet, and maybe wouldn't. Maybe it wasn't even the same truck. There wasn't much for her to call in. She and Declan didn't need backup.

Not yet.

Declan took the next street, even though his hotel was another five minutes down the highway. Drawing out the truck driver?

Sure enough the tan truck followed. Portia did the same, keeping her distance so they didn't look like a convoy. That would be too obvious. As it was, Declan had slowed.

Portia's phone rang, lighting up the dash display. She tapped the screen and the ringing in the car speakers switched to the low drone of tires on the road.

"Special Agent Finch."

"It's Declan."

She lifted her eyebrows at his number on the screen. Before she could say anything else, he said, "Listen, I'm on my way to the hotel, *like I said*." He paused. "But there's a tan truck behind me."

Apparently he felt the need to impress on her the fact he was doing what he'd told her he would this time. But instead of commenting on that, she said, "I'm behind the truck, on your six."

He was a smart man with training. He'd get the military reference, meaning she was directly behind him.

Silence filled the line.

"You're welcome." She laced the words with all the frustration this man brought out in her. Why was that? She didn't care about Declan Stringer enough for him to rub her the wrong way to this extent. Not after only knowing him for a few hours.

"Of course you are." More silence. Then, "I guess you should brace yourself."

"What—" She didn't get to finish before Declan's car brakes came on. He pulled up sharply, and the back end of his car swung out in a wide arc. When he was almost nose to nose with the truck, she saw the whites of Declan's teeth flash in the truck's headlights.

The man was crazy. He'd deliberately confronted the truck driver, not even knowing if it was the shooter. Declan could have just scared the life out of an innocent man who was only guilty of driving a tan-colored truck.

The truck driver hit the gas and pulled around Declan to speed off.

Declan's voice came through the car speakers. "Go get him."

Portia hung up. She was already doing what he ordered, even before his instruction. She wasn't going to give him the satisfaction of acquiescing over the phone. Not after the stunt he'd just pulled. Besides, hanging up on someone was just so satisfying.

She drove after the truck, following reasonably close to see where he went. The person driving still hadn't actually done anything illegal. The truck took a right turn onto a side street. Portia followed for two more turns before he pulled back into traffic on the highway about a mile closer to the hotel.

The phone rang, echoing through her car speakers. She turned the volume down.

Changed lanes, tried to spot the truck.

It was too far ahead.

Another mile, and she realized she'd lost him. Whoever he was, killer or not, he was gone now. She couldn't call in local PD to assist when the driver hadn't even done anything, and her own team was too far away at this time of night.

Portia slammed the heel of her hand against the steering wheel. She made a U-turn at the next intersection and drove back to where Declan had made that move, her phone ringing in the speakers the entire time. She ignored it.

When she pulled up behind his car he was standing in the open driver's door, phone to his ear. He hung up and tossed the phone inside, onto the seat, then stalked toward her.

Why was he mad?

Portia swung out of the car and slammed the door with every ounce of frustration she felt.

"Why didn't you answer the phone?"

She moved right into his space, her bootheels bringing her to eye level with him and she thanked God for that bit of extra height. Normally she didn't much appreciate that fact about herself. But she was grateful she could face him almost nose to nose right now. "Why did you do that stupid maneuver?"

"You mean bring the situation to a head, rather than lead him to the hotel where I'm staying?" His loud voice was laced with sarcasm.

Portia met him beat for beat. "I meant pushing it. Acting rashly."

"You lost him, didn't you?"

"Because *you* forced him to break off."

"This isn't my fault," he said.

"Well it's hardly mine."

"Fine. Neither of us is at fault."

She folded her arms and stared at him. Did he think that absolved him of the stupidity of that overly flashy maneuver? "Do they teach those stunts at Secret Service school?"

"You didn't get that training?"

"Not the kind which involves stunt driving just to show off." And she was done with this yelling match on the side of the road. "Did you get a license plate this time?"

He shook his head. "I couldn't see them. You?"

"No." She wanted to make a frustrated noise, but then he'd know this case was getting to her. Why couldn't anything in her life be easy? Why did it always feel like she was pushing a boulder uphill just to make it? God hadn't promised her easy days, but did it have to be *this hard*?

She sighed, realizing that might be why it had been so long since she'd prayed.

She said, "I'll follow you to your hotel."

"I don't need a babysitter."

She wasn't even going to respond to that. If he wanted to play the solitary hero, she would simply call it a free country—thank You, Lord—and follow him anyway. Because she had every right to be on the road.

It would just happen to be on the road right behind him.

Declan's eyes narrowed, as though he knew exactly what she was thinking. He wandered to his car and got in. Backing down? That didn't seem like him.

Portia called in what had happened as she followed him to the hotel. Maybe tomorrow she would wake up fresh—and a whole lot less frustrated with Declan Stringer.

At least, she prayed that would be the case.

Declan's phone rang just before eight the next morning. The screen of his phone switched from his Bible app to signify an incoming call. *Agent Finch.* He'd labeled her contact that to keep things professional between them. The phone vibrated across the surface of the diner booth table and clanged into his knife.

The night had been uneventful, and he'd occupied himself in those quiet hours constructing an email to his brother. He hadn't sent it. That conversation could come later, when he wasn't smack in the middle of a murder investigation. At least that was what he was telling himself. Plenty of self-denial going on here.

"Agent Stringer." His voice held that edge of frustration he'd been nursing since she lost the truck.

"It's Portia." Hers had the same tone. Either they were

destined to be best friends, or they'd part as sworn enemies.

"Didn't figure I'd hear from you this morning."

"Too bad. Rise and shine, cupcake." In the background, he could hear the muffled sounds of someone jostling keys. "Time to get to work."

He signaled the waitress. "Let me get the check. Where are we going?"

"The check? I thought you'd be sleeping in."

"I've been up since four. East Coast time, remember?" He handed the waitress a twenty and pushed his chair in before he strode to the door of the diner. "Went for a run. Took a shower, and then decided I needed an omelet."

"How nice for you. I've been in the office two hours already, running down leads and trying to figure out who tried to *kill you* yesterday."

"I didn't hit a trail, though I wanted to. Hotel gym."

"At least there's that." He heard the relief in her voice. She cared about him. Or she just didn't want to do the paperwork if he died.

"I'd much rather run outside." Before thinking about it, he added, "Maybe before I go home you'll show me a trail."

Silence. "Maybe."

"Don't like to run?"

"I'd be more concerned with whether or not you'll be able to keep up." Now there was an edge of a smile in her voice. Were they approaching friendly banter, or something else entirely?

Declan beeped the locks, and then climbed in the rental. "So where are we going?"

"The address listed on the John Doe's license was the one he rented under Nicholas's name. Squire ID'd him early this morning from his print. His name was Frank

Parsons. Was in the navy for a few years. He lived in Tacoma. You want to get a peek at his house?"

"Definitely." Frank Parsons had been killed pretending to be his brother, or someone with the name Nicholas Stringer. A close enough match physically that the killer likely thought he *was* Declan's brother. Maybe. There was a resemblance. He figured that was why Frank Parsons had been killed.

And why the killer had come after Declan. Twice.

The address Portia texted over had a unit number, which he figured was an apartment. When he pulled onto the street, the neighborhood took a significant downturn. Run-down buildings that looked to have been erected in the seventies, and maybe never updated. The parking spots had green corrugated metal roofs. Declan found a visitor's spot close to where the forensics van had parked, then climbed the stairs where neighbors had congregated.

He gave his information to the officer at the door and showed his badge. The officer said "Thanks."

The smell inside made him wrinkle his nose. "Agent Finch?" He didn't want to venture into every room. Not when certain ones smelled worse than the living room/kitchen/dining area.

She called back, "Second door on the left."

The first room had a double bed and rumpled covers. Two forensics guys were going over a dresser. He found Portia in the second room, what would've been an office or guest room in any other house. Frank Parsons had piled in there what most people would have thrown in a storage unit to keep it from cluttering up their place.

Boxes were stacked high. Trash bags bulged with papers, or clothes. A bike, a kayak and a dog crate were among the stacks. He even saw an ironing board.

"Whoa."

Portia looked up from a stack of papers. "Pretty much. Though, this actually makes life easier for us."

"Assuming he doesn't have a storage unit, or some other place, equally as packed with boxes that should all be labeled Miscellaneous."

She cracked a smile at that, then said, "I've managed to solve one mystery, at least."

"What's that?"

She pulled a paper from the pile and stepped over an overflowing bag of shoes and boots. "Frank Parsons owned a tan truck."

Declan felt his eyebrows lift. "And our mysterious gunman happens to be driving one?"

"Same make and model from last night."

He didn't want to get into an argument about that. "BOLO?"

She nodded. "Already sent the information across the wires. Now all we need is for local police, or one of our people, to spot the truck."

Hopefully with the gunman in it. Or close by, so they could nab him. The fact they were able to alert all law enforcement to "be on the lookout" for their truck could mean the difference between the shooter finding them, or their finding him first.

"I'm going to get this to the techs so they can bag it up." She wandered out, and he went over to the stack she'd been working on.

A minute later gunshots rang out, followed immediately by the shattering of glass.

FIVE

The first shot blew a hole in the evidence bag she was holding. In the seconds while the shooter reloaded, Portia dived behind the couch. The crime scene technician did the same, taking cover behind a battered recliner. Water rushed in her ears, the adrenaline eclipsing everything else so that she could only hear muffled yelling.

Portia looked at the tattered remnants of the evidence bag, then called out to the tech. “Lewson?”

The tech didn’t answer her.

“If we stay here, we’re going to get killed by that sniper.”

If she had to, she would force him to move. A round like the ones the shooter had loaded into his rifle would blow a hole in the couch she was hiding behind. Then again, if they ran for it would they get picked off as they tried to escape the kill zone?

She pulled her phone out and called in their location, letting the dispatcher know shots had been fired. They didn’t need an ambulance right now, but things could change in a matter of seconds during a situation like this. Portia stowed her phone.

“I know,” Lewson whimpered. “Put Mom on the phone.”

She glanced at the technician and found he was on

his own call. The guy was younger than she'd thought at first—younger than Chris.

A shot hit the wall behind them.

"Just do it!" A tear ran down his face.

She should say something to reassure him. Maybe crawl over there. Portia lifted up a couple of inches and peered over the couch.

"Are you crazy?" Declan's voice was a whisper, but he was mad. "Get down." He crouch-walked down the hall, face tight. A dark look in his eyes. Gun ready. "You're going to get your head blown off."

She wasn't taking any risk she wasn't completely okay with. All of their lives were at stake right now—not just hers. This wasn't about protecting herself. "I'm trying to see where the shots are coming from."

"You called it in?"

She nodded as he crowded against the back of the couch right beside her. His eyelashes were really that long? His gaze caught hers, and they stared at each other for a second.

Portia glanced away. "Cops will be here in a second, and then we can get out of here."

She heard a hitch of breath. It wasn't Declan's, though.

"I don't know if I'm going to make it." Beyond Declan the technician said, "I just wanted to tell you I appreciate everything you've done for me."

Portia looked over the Secret Service agent's shoulder to see Lewson.

"Bye, Mom." He hung up the phone swiping away tears and trying to hold it together.

"We're going to be okay, Lewson," she said to him. "Police and NCIS are on their way." This situation meant armed response agents, basically their version of SWAT.

So long as the three of them stayed out of sight, the

shooter wasn't going to be given a target. He wouldn't be able to pick them off before help got there.

Lewson lowered the phone, eyes wide. Flushed. He looked to the door, then around the room not meeting her eyes. What was he…

The guy got up, his breath already coming in heaves even before he started to make a run for it. He jumped up and headed for the door with his arms and legs pumping.

"No," she yelled after him. "Don't—"

A shot rang out.

The technician dropped to the floor, clutching his shoulder. He cried out. Blood damped the shirt beneath his fingers.

Portia reached out her arm, trying to grasp the guy's shoe with her fingers. She kept the rest of her body behind the couch.

"Careful."

Like she needed Declan to tell her that? She was perfectly capable of keeping herself safe. She'd been doing it for more than thirty years already. She hardly needed his help all of a sudden. She wasn't even the gunman's target.

Portia got enough of a grip on the shoe she could pull it toward her. When Lewson was close enough, Declan helped, as well. Together they got the technician behind the couch with them, his body half on the carpet and half on the linoleum of the dining area where a card table and two folding chairs stood.

In the distance, the sound of sirens approached their location.

"Help is on the way." Why she needed to say that aloud, she didn't know. Reassuring herself, probably. She didn't have time to think on it. Not with Lewson bleeding on the floor.

Portia hooked two fingers in the tear in the technician's

jacket and pulled it away from the skin. She ripped the material far enough that she could slip the sleeve from his arm, then balled it up and pressed it against the wound.

The technician groaned. Beside them, Declan called in the need for an ambulance.

"Won't be long," she said. "We'll get you help."

Declan hung up. "No more shots."

Portia kept her focus on the injured man, offering a smile to reassure him that she thought he wouldn't die from this. "You think he left?"

"Took his shots, then heard the sirens. I wouldn't stick around."

The technician gasped. "So he's gone?"

Declan said, "It's what I'd do. No use waiting too long and getting cornered by cops."

Portia nodded to the tech. "That means the ambulance won't be far behind."

"I'm gonna be okay?"

Portia had no idea. "You're conscious, that's good. The EMTs will get you to hospital, and the doctors can patch you right up."

Out the corner of her eye she saw Declan glance at her. Did he know she was just saying all this to make the guy feel better and not lose it? She needed Lewson to keep hanging on until help got there. She could command her team. Stressful situations weren't a problem. But Portia could not deal when people starting sniffling and crying, carrying on about how it was all over. There was no antidote to hopelessness—at least nothing she could say that would stop the tears.

Her dad hadn't known what to do when she cried. Tears were unacceptable, unless they were flowing because she was spitting mad. Now she always got tongue-tied when people were upset.

"Tacoma Police Department!"

Portia yelled back, "All clear!"

Two cops strode in, guns drawn. They saw the scene and stowed their weapons.

She said, "The shooting stopped."

One of the officers waved in EMTs, carrying their bulky bags and a backboard between them. They rushed to the technician, and Portia got out of the way.

"I'm going to look for the shooter." Declan strode to the door.

Before she could say anything, he disappeared. Portia glanced at the cop like they'd planned this whole thing and not like Declan was going off half-cocked again. "Call if you need anything. You have people going after the shooter?"

The cop nodded. "Don't get in their way."

Before they could get in a turf war, Portia headed out after Declan. She wasn't about to waste time explaining the fact this was definitely her case. The police were only there to assist in tracking down the shooter.

It was up to her to make sure the killer didn't get anywhere near Declan.

He heard her follow, and it didn't surprise him. Portia wasn't the kind of woman who hung back when there was a gunman to find.

Declan passed the handful of cop cars and stepped into the street first. Portia caught up, and they raced together to the other side. Cops peppered the sidewalks to the north and south of the street and had congregated around the entrance of an apartment building across from Frank Parsons's place.

Declan flashed his badge. "In there?"

The cop started, mouth open. He'd never seen a fed before? That wasn't possible. Still the man's face remained blank, like he had no idea what to say about the fact there was a Secret Service agent in the mix of things.

"He's with me, Sergeant."

The man nodded. "Agent Finch." He held the door open. "Lieutenant Milton is upstairs."

Portia nudged Declan's back. He took that as his cue to head inside and stepped aside for her to go first.

Big mistake.

She swept past him, thunder in her eyes. The cops standing around the entrance reacted, but it was subtle. The curling up of a lip. A cough. Nervous shifting of a stance. Declan glanced at the sergeant.

The man said, "Happy hunting."

Declan followed Portia, wondering if the man was talking about the search for the gunman, or something to do with Portia. Working in this area, even as a federal agent, she would have a professional relationship with police. She clearly knew that sergeant. They were in Tacoma, not Seattle, and not close to the navy base, but he figured she was a memorable woman. And evidently these guys thought she was a force to be reckoned with.

"What was that?"

He was so in his own thoughts he nearly ran into her. Declan sputtered for a second, then said, "Me being a gentleman?"

"That's what you call it?"

"Maybe it's in short supply these days." But he proved it wasn't gone from the world because he pulled the door to the stairwell open for her. "That doesn't mean I can't break the mold."

She eyed him, then walked through the door. Up the stairs.

At the access door to the roof she turned back to him.

"Break the mold?" It was like she didn't know whether to laugh or get mad. Probably because she thought he was ridiculous.

Declan grinned and lifted his chin. "I try." Then he said, "Ready to go see where this guy shot from?"

She nodded and stepped out onto the building's roof. Slightly more upscale than the residences across the street, but that wasn't saying much. Portia introduced him around to the cops on-scene, and they walked the space.

The shooter was long gone, the place now crawling with police. Declan figured he was right to have assumed the gunman heard the sirens and decided it was safer to cut and run. Live to fight another day.

Portia stood at the edge of the roof, her attention on Frank Parsons's apartment. Declan surveyed the rooftop, leaving her to her thoughts. She would tell him when she was ready. Or not. He was learning that this woman was independent and capable. When she needed something, would she ask? If she turned out to be just as stubborn as he was—which he considered highly likely at this point—they might end up butting heads at every step of this case.

"What are you thinking?"

He smiled at her question.

"Maybe I don't want to know."

Declan laughed. "Nothing special." At least, nothing he was willing to admit to at this stage of whatever they were having. Certainly not a relationship. That wasn't part of his future—not when he'd have to keep the truth about his family history from the person he was having a relationship with. "I'm glad the technician is going to be okay, and that no one else got hurt."

"Me too." But her humor from a second ago had dissipated now. Her gaze flicked back to the apartment they'd been in when the shooting started. "I don't like being in someone's crosshairs."

He saw the shiver that moved through her. Declan wanted to put his hand on her shoulder. Would she accept that? Portia seemed determined to be alone—in everything. Even with the obvious connection she had with her team she remained slightly removed.

"We'll find him."

"Before or after he kills you?"

"I don't need protecting, Portia."

This might be the first time the threat directed at him was personal—or so their theory went. But he was trained. He didn't need a protective detail. Declan *was* the protective detail.

"At the White House you have infrastructure in place for security, right?"

Declan nodded.

"Is that same infrastructure in place in your hotel room? Or here on this rooftop?"

"I don't need a team of local LEOs thinking they're helping by sitting in a black-and-white outside wherever I'm at."

"The cops—"

He shook his head. "Don't compare them to the president's protective detail, because I'm not going to buy it."

"He shot at me and the tech. You weren't even in the room." She pinned him with a look. "Are you willing to put someone else's death on your conscience? It went okay for the tech today, but we might not get away with only minor injuries next time."

Declan didn't want the guilt of a death on his conscience. That wasn't what he figured he'd leave this investigation with. They needed to find the man who'd shot Frank Parsons. Then Declan could go back to DC with only the fond memory of Portia Finch. That spark, the connection he was feeling between them right now.

He watched her nose wrinkle slightly. She said, "What—"

"Special Agent Finch."

They both looked over. The police lieutenant said, "We have something."

No recrimination on his face. It was like the man didn't even know something had been happening between them just now.

Declan shook his head and followed Portia over to where the officer stood. Another cop was crouched, taking pictures. She deposited whatever they'd found in an evidence bag and held it up.

Portia took the bag, holding it close enough they could both see the shell casing.

"He didn't have time to police his brass," Declan said aloud even as he realized it.

"That's what I'm thinking."

Shell casings could be traced. The bullets were across the street in the apartment where the technician had been shot. Over here, the shooter evidently hadn't had time to do more than grab his weapon and run. Certainly not enough time to pick up the evidence he'd left behind.

"So either he was in a hurry and got sloppy—"

Portia said, "And how likely is that?"

"—or the shooter knew the casings couldn't be traced back to incriminate him."

"He didn't hit either of us. He missed."

"And the technician got winged. So you're going to vote for him being sloppy?"

She motioned to the evidence bag. "It's a theory. I just don't get why he shot at us in the woods and then followed you—both of which involved the tan truck—and now he's a sniper?"

"The change of MO."

"It doesn't make sense. Snipers are good…or at least usually better than this."

Declan didn't like that thought. "So he missed on purpose? He isn't trying to kill me?"

"Or this was a different shooter," she said. "Someone trying to warn us things are getting dangerous. That we're getting close."

He wasn't sure if she thought that was a good or bad thing. Maybe both.

Declan was nervous either way. But he wasn't going to let Portia in on that fact. Her phone rang. She answered it and started to turn away. Then spun back, her gaze on him again.

"We'll be right there."

SIX

The elevator doors swung open and Portia strode out, glad to escape the confines of that metal box she normally considered a source of quiet space. Having Declan in there made the thing feel so much smaller.

He was just so...*compelling* probably wasn't the right word, but it fit. First he'd been a stranger. Now having him with her had begun to feel almost normal. Almost. At this rate she was going to get used to him. Then he'd be gone, and it would be just her again.

Alone.

That way was better. She knew how to be alone. She understood how it worked when she could go where she wanted and do what she wanted whenever. She didn't have to answer to anyone. And yes, she knew marriage wasn't this trap where she'd have to tell the other person everything she was doing like she needed their permission. But Portia had been single for a long time, and she liked it. Changing would require giving up some of the freedom she'd been enjoying.

Portia pressed the button and heard the buzzer ring in the forensics lab. A few seconds later Squire came into view. Barely twenty years old, he wore a white lab coat, underneath which were a comic book T-shirt, skinny jeans and Converse sneakers. His hair was bright red and stood up like he'd gotten an electric shock.

"Whoa." Declan coughed to cover his reaction.

Portia grinned at Squire and held up the bag of sour candy she'd stopped at a gas station for. His eyes widened, and he opened the door.

Portia said, "Only the best for you."

"Gimme gimme."

Before she could roll her eyes, Squire noticed Declan. "The brother?"

Portia nodded, handing over the bagged candy.

Squire said, "I'd shake your hand, but you'd be a biohazard for the next thirteen hours."

Declan cracked a smile. "Nice to meet you."

"You too. At least until I tell you what I found, then your opinion might change." Squire turned and swept into his lab. The white coat billowed behind him along with the sound of crackling candy bag. He tossed a handful in his mouth and grabbed the levers on the sides of his desk to lift it to standing height.

Portia typed fast, but when Squire's fingers hit the keys he made her look like a finger pecker. Declan started to speak. Portia motioned to him, then pressed her index finger to her lips. They waited for Squire to be finished.

The kid likely didn't know they'd been shot at in Frank Parsons's apartment. Not that he was oblivious to the real world; he simply preferred his lab. Things he could quantify—which didn't include people, or their emotions. She appreciated that about him. Life was much simpler if it could be controlled. Even if the effort might be futile.

"The bullet from the tree was a bust. Too squashed. The one pulled from Frank Parsons during autopsy, however, different story. I ran it through all our databases—and some I'm not supposed to have access to—and got a match." He glanced at Declan. "Irregularities inside the gun barrel mean that when it's fired, the bullet basically gets scratched. It creates striations on the bullet so we can match rounds that came from the same gun."

Portia figured Declan probably knew all that, but the kid was a good teacher in her opinion. And their Secret Service agent friend didn't seem to mind the refresher course. He said, "And you found a match to the bullet that killed Frank Parsons?"

"It's a cold case from a few years ago."

Portia's stomach sank as she realized that whatever Squire was about to tell her, she wasn't going to like. That was why he'd started with the forensics lesson—not for Declan's benefit.

She said, "Squire, whose murder does the bullet match?"

It was Declan who answered. "My father's."

She turned to Declan and felt her eyes widen. "Your—"

Squire said, "He's right. The murder of Thomas Harris went unsolved."

Portia blew out a breath. "Until now."

Declan's gaze settled on her. "Now?"

"Our suspect. There's no way he bought that gun from some stranger, and then just *happened* to murder a man with your brother's ID."

Though Portia would guess, when they finally brought this guy in for questioning, that would be exactly what he said. Every suspect she'd ever sat across that interview table from started their explanation with trying to explain they were nowhere near the crime. And had nothing to do with it. Don't even know any of the people involved.

That was why their evidence had to be conclusive.

Declan said, "So do you think it's connected to Nicholas and me?"

She nodded. "Coincidence can't do that. This man targeted you. Whether or not he's the one who pulled the trigger on your father, I'd guess he knows who did. And he evidently has a vested interest in you and your brother also being dead."

Declan glanced down and rubbed strong fingers along his jaw. Portia left him to his thoughts and turned to Squire. "Anything else pressing?"

He shook his head. "I'll email you the full report."

"Thank you." She turned back to the Secret Service agent. "Declan?"

They moved out of the lab, back to the elevator. When the doors slid shut she turned to him. There were only seconds before they reached the floor where her office was. Doing a quick assessment of his state of mind, she said, "Coffee?" With all that had happened at the apartment, they'd skipped lunch. But it was always time for caffeine.

Relief washed over his face. "Coffee would be good."

If there was anything written on her face, he either didn't mention it or was so far in his own head he didn't notice. She couldn't imagine what it would've been like to have a criminal for a father.

Or to have a father who was murdered.

She and her dad had clicked like two pieces of the same puzzle. Their lives had synchronized, probably in part because her dad had been a marine. But also because they'd both appreciated the simplicity of routine. They'd lived comfortably, sharing warmth in the silence while they ate or watched TV. Hiking on the weekend. Kayaking. Fishing on her dad's boat.

When he'd gotten sick, she'd wheeled him onto the boat and taken him out to sea so he could feel the ocean wind on his face.

Tears gathered in her eyes, stinging hot. Portia glanced up at the ceiling of the elevator and blinked them away before the worst happened. When the doors slid open, she strode out like there was nothing wrong. No one needed to know what had happened. The way her father had chosen to end his life. She'd given the police everything they'd needed and had sat down with the director to explain.

She bit her lip and headed for the break room. At the door she glanced back to check Declan was with her. He strode along behind, his attention on his phone. He frowned, then stowed the device in his pocket. Gave her a tiny smile.

This wasn't about her, or her unresolved emotions over her father's end. Portia needed to put that aside. To *keep* pushing it aside until she was ready to have that conversation with herself.

For now, all she needed to worry about was the fact that while Declan had mentioned his father's death, she couldn't help feeling like there might be more to the story. After all, when he'd first told her the story he'd neglected to tell her that his father had been murdered.

Which just gave her more reason to keep things professional between them. She didn't need to get in a relationship with someone who had as many father issues as she did. There was a mess waiting to happen.

Maybe when she retired from NCIS she would find a nice, quiet man with no issues. There was probably one out there somewhere, right?

She poured two mugs, doctored them with cream and motioned for Declan to sit. She did the same, took a sip and then said, "I think it's time for you to tell me exactly how your father was murdered."

* * *

Declan left his mug untouched and shut his eyes. Too much was swimming around in his head. Memories. Emotions. He could hardly pin one down long enough to actually process it. Let alone work through everything in order to clear his head.

He felt her hand touch his, her fingers warm from her own coffee mug. She didn't say anything, just let him be. Let him talk when he was ready to. Even the counselor he'd seen for a long time asked questions. Pulled the information—and the feelings—out of him. Portia simply let him be who he was.

"He didn't show up to meet me because..." Declan opened his eyes and looked at her, unable to even say it. "The cops showed up a couple of days later to let us know he was gone."

Her face softened.

"Shot. Dumped in the woods, found by a hiker. Sound familiar?" He'd read the file a few years ago and called the investigating detective. The man had retired since and didn't have much to say. Especially to someone he called kid despite the fact Declan had been a grown man when they spoke.

He said, "A dead criminal. No leads. Once he was buried, the investigation seemed to stall out. They probably had more important cases to take care of. My aunt, who we went to live with after he went to prison, told me back then that I should move on. Nicholas didn't want to talk about it. It seemed better to let it all go. To forget."

Her fingers slipped from his, and she sat back. Took a sip of her coffee. Shut down. What was that about? He didn't have time to ask before she said, "Tell me everything you know about his death."

Declan blew out a breath and told her what the detective had said. "I always figured it was someone after revenge. He hadn't been out of prison all that long. Good behavior." How true that was, he didn't know. "No physical evidence beyond the gunshot. Rain washed the majority of the earth and the body between the time he was killed—or his body dumped—and when he was found."

She nodded again, and he saw something that looked a whole lot like sympathy. Maybe guilt.

"I never thought this would come back around. Everyone said forget about it and move on. Now someone tries to kill Nicholas? Thankfully, he was out of the country." Declan wiped his hands down his face. Despite their strained relationship, he didn't want to know how it would feel if his only remaining sibling was killed. He loved his aunt and uncle. They'd taken Declan and Nicholas in after their father had been arrested. But nothing was closer than the bond between two brothers.

And yet, his brother was in danger every day as a marine. So why had it only hit him *now* that Nick's death would leave a hole in his life? Declan had been a subpar big brother, by any standard of measurement. Nick didn't want much to do with him, but that didn't mean Declan couldn't at least try to get some kind of dialogue going between them. They were all each other had for immediate family. Didn't that count for something?

If the worst happened to Declan would his brother even care?

Before he could fall into that spiral of depressing thoughts, he drank half his coffee down then said, "Does Squire know anything about our shooter?"

"Just the gun connection." Portia eyed him. "Think you can get us a list of possible enemies who might want revenge against you for what your father did?"

"Not sure how much I know. It's all from the police report, and newspaper files. You guys can probably look up that stuff and find the information better than I can piece it together from memory."

She nodded. "Okay." Giving him a look that said she might approve of his suggestion. No one wanted to be going on incomplete information. He wasn't an investigator, whereas Portia and her team were. Theirs was an interesting job, seeing so much death and expending energy to unravel the mystery of it.

Declan much preferred the minute-to-minute watchfulness of protecting the president. That was frontline stuff. Kind of like what Nick did with the marines. His job was first line, offense. Not playing defense, or even catch-up like these agents did. They came in after the action. He'd rather be there when it happened.

He respected the job they did, even if he didn't think he could do it himself.

"Anything else?" His coffee cup was empty now.

Portia's face blanked. "There's a gunman after you. One who has been after your family for years."

"There have been plenty of opportunities. And yet he's waited until now."

"So you figure he isn't in a hurry, even though he shot at you twice in as many days?"

Declan said, "The sniper might have been someone else. We can only link Parsons's death to my father's."

"You still need protection, Declan."

"Maybe I should just go back to Washington. There's plenty of protection at the White House."

"You'd bring a killer back there with you? Surrounded by tourists and important people who shouldn't be in a killer's crosshairs?"

Declan said, "No one should be in a killer's crosshairs." A thought occurred to him. "But you'd rather it was you."

Portia stared him down. "Why not? I can take care of myself."

"But I can't? I need protection?"

"You're the intended target."

"So I'll watch my back. And I'm good with you, or your team, with me. But I'm not about to turn my life upside down because of a threat. I'm not going to run and hide. Not when this has gone on for years. This man stuck around to shoot at me, hours after he thought he'd killed Nicholas."

"He was trying to draw you out."

Declan shrugged. "Probably. But I'm not going to let him kill me." He thought back to that day. "You winged him. Maybe he's laying low because he's injured."

Portia got up and wandered to the break room sink where she rinsed out her mug. "Injured or not, there's a sniper out there, as well." She turned and leaned her hips against the counter. "You're sticking around?"

"I want to know who it is that killed a man he thought was Nicholas, and who likely killed my dad, as well."

She nodded. "I understand."

But she didn't like it. "You'd rather I left? Or you'd just rather I sat in a safe house for the next three days of my vacation while *you* figure this out?"

One corner of her mouth curled up. "I can dream."

Declan felt himself smile. "At least you have realistic expectations."

She chuckled. She knew he'd never have sat in a safe house. He wasn't the kind of person to be idle when the threat was active—a threat against him. One of her teammates, Lenny, stuck his head in the door, eyes wide at the sight of Portia laughing. “Local cops found the truck. They’re in pursuit.”

“Tell them to hold back. Declan and I will catch up.”

“Declan?”

He turned to Lenny in time to see it wasn’t frustration or disapproval in his tone. Still more surprise—like with the laughter.

Portia said, “Special Agent Stringer and I are heading out. Pass the word out to the cops.”

Lenny nodded. “Copy that.”

Bremerton to Seattle was a ferry ride away, but Portia made good time. They got word from the cops that the truck had parked outside a convenience store in Georgetown ten minutes ago and pulled over behind it. A few minutes later a man left the store with a plastic grocery bag dangling from one hand. Grizzled, wearing boots, jeans and a bulky jacket, his dingy ball cap was pulled low.

Declan cracked the door and strode over, the stress of the last few days filling his mind. This man had shot at him. He’d determined to kill someone he thought was Nick. There was no way Declan would allow him to escape this time.

“Hey!”

The grizzled man blanched. Dropped his bag.

Turned.

And ran.

SEVEN

"NCIS!"

It was too late. The guy loped away, picking up speed as he moved. Declan raced after the suspect. Portia held her gun in a tight grip and followed. People around them screamed and ran away from the fuss. There was nothing she could do except follow. Make sure Declan didn't get himself killed—or do anything else stupid.

Portia thought over what she knew of this part of Tacoma and ducked right to head down the next street. Two buildings over she moved north between the tiny storefronts that kind of looked like dominoes to her. If she was correct, the gunman would take a right up ahead and she could come out in front of him.

If she was fast enough.

Portia wanted to pray that nothing happened between Declan and the gunman while she wasn't with him, but would it even help? Right before the end of her father's life, she'd been drawn in to his move toward more prayer and what would come after this life. Once he was gone, she'd let that go along with him.

Portia pumped her arms and legs like this was the one-hundred-meter sprint. Pushed her body as hard as she could to gain ground. That was the only way she'd come out ahead of Declan and the suspect.

Two teens rounded the corner ahead of her. The girl squealed, and they ducked out of her way. Whether they saw her badge or not, she didn't have time to figure out. Or explain who she was. What she was doing.

Portia emerged from between the buildings and headed left. She wouldn't know her plan had worked until—

The grizzled man raced around the corner, right toward her. Portia planted her feet and held her gun up. "NCIS. Stop."

His eyes were glazed. He didn't stop. She gave the command again, but it was too late. He barreled into her. Portia landed on her back. All the breath left her in a rush. She heard Declan yell, and she pushed at the man. Tried to use his momentum to roll them both. But it was no use when the guy was this huge and heavy.

He didn't go for the gun, now pressed sideways against his chest between her hand and his shirt, but he had to feel it. She shoved at him again, but he didn't move from her. She pulled out her arm and used the gun to hit him on the head.

Portia bent one knee, planted her foot and then rolled with every bit of strength she had. The man was dazed enough from her hit that she got him on his back. She knelt upright beside him and held her gun where he'd make no mistake as to her intentions.

Declan stood beside them in a similar stance.

"Hands up." She waited for him to comply, then said, "Declan?"

"I've got you covered."

Portia stowed her weapon. She patted the man down, then flipped him on his stomach and did the same to that side. The last thing she needed was for him to pull a weapon from behind his back.

She was cautious of the fact he might have a gunshot wound in his shoulder or arm, but he never reacted to her tugging his arms behind his back to secure them so she could pat him down.

She stood. “Okay, up. We need to talk.”

“What did I do?” His words were slurred enough she wondered that he’d even been able to walk straight, let alone run.

“Apart from shoot at us and follow Agent Stringer in that truck of yours?” She sucked in air, still out of breath from that hard sprint. “I’m guessing…former military. Maybe a sniper?” If he wasn’t the shooter from the woods that had to mean he was their sniper.

Police sirens echoed through the neighborhood. They were probably headed to the truck, and Portia’s car that she’d double-parked.

“Sniper…*wha*…?”

Portia held his arm and led him back toward the car, seeing that he wasn’t as old as his weathered appearance suggested. “You know exactly what you did. So who are you? You’re not old enough that Thomas Harris swindled you. So I’m guessing…your parents?”

The grizzled man glanced at her over his shoulder. Then at Declan, holding his gun aimed at the man as they walked. Just in case. The suspect’s eyes narrowed.

“Careful.” She didn’t want him tripping over his feet.

“You think I’m *who* now?” His eyes were a little clearer but moved constantly. Like he didn’t know where to focus.

Portia had to entertain the possibility he wasn’t either of the two men—if there were two—that they were looking for. The truck could be the wrong truck, considering they didn’t have a license plate. The truck this man had been driving had no plates. Could just be coincidence, but did she believe that? Not really.

That left the option that it was the right truck, but the wrong man.

"You have a name?" she asked.

"Wallace."

"That your last name, or first name?"

He hesitated, gaze on the street in front of them. "Not much cause for a last name in my circles."

Portia surveyed the clothes he wore. Ragged at the edges. He had at least two layers of shirt on, maybe more than that. Cargo pants. Probably layers underneath, judging by how bulky they were.

"How long you been on the streets?"

"Too long." Sniff.

"How'd you get the truck?" Not to mention the money, though he'd likely get testy—and possibly shut down—if she asked about the windfall that'd led him to shopping at the corner store.

"Guy gave me two hundred and the keys. Told me to drive it around until tomorrow morning, then dump it." He shrugged one shoulder. "No skin off my nose."

"I've never understood that expression." She gave him a smile. "I mean, skin off my nose…ouch." She rubbed her nose.

He chuckled, a low rumbling sound. Still didn't meet her eyes.

"Think you can describe the man?"

He said, "Six foot, maybe. Gray hair. Built. Tanned. Wasn't wearing a jacket."

"Think you can remember enough to tell a sketch artist?"

"I remember his arms."

Given his lack of eye contact so far, she figured he

was right. He wouldn't be able to give them much more than he already had. "Tattoos?" If he was military, they could lead Portia to the man's identity.

He shrugged. Not a yes, not a no.

Police cars lined the street, the cops spread out and asking witnesses what had happened. One turned, saw the three of them approaching and pointed.

"You'll likely have to give the cops your last name," she said. "It'll clear this up faster than anything else if we can run your ID and prove you don't have a connection to this."

If he had no relationship to anyone Declan's father had swindled it meant the man had no motive to murder.

He studied her. "I'll tell them about the man who gave me the truck, but I'm keeping the money."

She nodded. He probably needed it.

Portia got him situated with the cops so they could get all the information they could from him. Then she pulled the sergeant who'd arrived on-scene aside and had a word about what they were going to do with the man when they were done questioning him. She didn't want them mistakenly arresting him for stealing the truck.

Declan watched as Portia handled the homeless man until he was smiling at her and went with the cops like that was the natural thing to do. How she'd managed to turn the conversation around from the man being hostile, to amicable, he didn't know. Even having watched the interchange himself.

When she walked back over he said, "That was good work. I wouldn't have pegged him for an innocent who'd been pulled in unawares."

Portia's brow crinkled, and she looked up at the rooftops of the buildings around them. "Innocent is up for debate, since we don't know for sure I was right." She glanced at him, then went back to scanning their immediate area. "But it's a solid guess he's not partners with the killer and lying to us about it. I'd just rather he remembered the guy's face. Even a little bit."

"Agreed," he said. "Now tell me what has you spooked."

She looked at him. Something in her eyes made him want to protect her. To watch her back like she was one of his protectees. He saw the moment she recognized that in him, and her eyes narrowed. "Just checking for a sniper."

"Good idea." They had been shot at by a rifle earlier that morning, at Frank Parsons's apartment. Whoever it was could be targeting them now, as well. "Do we head back to the office?"

She shook her head. "Let's check out the truck first." But she spoke to one of the officers and pointed up at the buildings around them. The officer nodded, then moved off.

After what he'd just seen of Portia's expertise, he was content to follow her lead. They still didn't know if the man in the truck and their sniper were one and the same.

He cracked the driver's door on the truck while she opened the passenger's side. Nothing on the seat. Keys in the ignition, where presumably the homeless guy had left them before he went in the store. No personal attachment to the vehicle, and he didn't much care if it got stolen while he was in the corner store.

Declan wasn't convinced their gunman had paid the homeless man to drive the truck around before dumping it. He wasn't sure if he could take the man's word for it. He checked the footwell, and under the seat. "Does it seem clean to you?"

Portia wrinkled her nose, her attention focused on the center console. Declan leaned the seat forward and looked behind it. An old road map, probably outdated now. No wrappers, or other trash. Not even any receipts from gas stations in the driver's door pocket.

"What's weird with this picture?" He just couldn't put his finger on what it was, since he wasn't finding anything. Maybe that was it. The *lack* accounting for more than the presence of something that might help them.

Portia straightened. "We'll get the truck towed to the office. I'm sure Squire will find what we're missing."

"That's the point." The idea coalesced as he put together what he was seeing. Or, more to the point, what he *wasn't*. "There isn't even any dust in here. And I get clearing out everything so you don't leave behind any evidence, but this was overkill. He wiped down the dash. And I'm guessing even Squire isn't going to find any stray hairs in here. Before he handed the keys over to that guy, our killer covered his tracks in a major way."

Declan said, "If he paid the guy to drive the truck, then he wanted it moving. To push off the timeline of when it would be found."

"Rather than hide it somewhere?"

"Maybe he didn't have anywhere to put it. But what he did do was make sure all traces of anything were gone. I'm guessing even your forensic technician is going to have a hard time finding physical evidence that's going to lead you back to this guy."

She frowned, then clicked the latch to flip down the glove box. A handgun had been stuffed inside, with the usual collection of papers he figured everyone kept in there along with their vehicle registration.

"Huh."

"A gift for us?"

"If he didn't so much as leave a hair," Portia said, "but he left a gun behind, then there's a reason for it."

Declan circled the car while she used a gloved hand to place the weapon in a plastic evidence bag. She sealed the end and made a notation on the bag. He got out his phone and made a note of the gun's serial number.

She had contacts, but so did he. Maybe his people could run this gun faster or maybe not, but they needed everything they could get right now.

She said, "Let's get this back to the office."

Declan nodded, and they headed for her car. Midway she pulled out her phone, then juggled that and the bag while she pulled out her keys. She tossed them to him. "You drive. My emails are going crazy."

He snatched the keys in midair and clicked the locks. "I know what that's like."

Constant updates. Briefings. Meetings. Seminars. Training. His life was like rolling back just to get hit again, left hook. Right hook. Dodge. The moment he tried to make a swing something else would pop up in the way and he'd have to account for that.

Before he got in the car, Declan looked around him. This city wasn't all that different, except for the ocean of trees scattered throughout. There were mountains everywhere he looked in this part of the country. The phrase *breath of fresh air* came to mind. He could breathe out here. Not crowded in by work, work and then more work.

Things hadn't been any less stressful here. But for some reason it felt…easier? He didn't even know how to describe it. Not really. He might be on vacation, but nothing that had happened since his plane landed at Sea-Tac was vacation-like.

The driver's door opened, pushing against his stomach. Portia leaned over the center console. "Are we going?"

He nodded and got in, following the directions given

by the GPS on her dash. Once they were on the highway headed back to the base—rather than taking the ferry again—Declan was finally about to relax and enjoy the drive.

Then he noticed the car behind them.

Declan opened his mouth to tell Portia but held off. What if it was nothing…okay, so it probably wasn't nothing. Not given the last couple of days they'd had. Still, he kept an eye on their tail, and left Portia to her work for a minute.

When the car's driver hit the gas and began to come up behind them in an aggressive manner, he tapped her arm. "Hold on."

Declan cut right across two lanes, hit the rumble strip for a second and straightened the car back into the slow lane.

She said, "What is it?" But turned to look out the back window.

The car that had been behind them in the fast lane did the same.

Portia said, "The blue Taurus?"

Declan nodded. "Yep."

"Well, I have to say I prefer a car chase to a sniper."

Declan nearly smiled. Nearly. Last time he'd pushed the situation, and they'd ended up losing the guy.

Before he could come up with a plan, the car picked up speed again and rammed them. Declan's seat belt locked. Portia made an *oof* sound.

"You good?"

She nodded, typing on her phone. "I'll get the message to state troopers. What was the last mile marker you saw?"

He told her the number.

The car behind clipped their back bumper. Portia's car

fishtailed, then started to spin. He gripped the wheel and tried to counteract but got no traction.

They crossed the rumble strip, onto the hard shoulder. Then grass. Ten feet later they slammed into a tree and the airbags blew.

Declan blinked and tried to focus. How long had he been unconscious? He pushed at the airbag and tried to breathe past the smell. Portia was slumped against the door on her side. He touched the far side of her face and his fingers came back bloody. She'd hit her head.

And the evidence bag containing the gun was gone.

EIGHT

Portia flicked her hair forward to cover the little bandage on the right side of her temple. She checked her reflection in the elevator to make sure it was concealed. She'd taken a couple of pain pills, so the headache wasn't too bad.

Beyond her in the reflection, Declan observed the action. Portia turned back to the doors. Before he could say anything, they reached their floor. The doors opened, and she strode out, along the perimeter of the room to her team's desks.

"What's the latest?" she asked, rounding the corner into the middle of their little huddle.

Lenny, Anna and Chris all stood. Lenny said, "Are you okay?"

Portia waved away their concern, even though half an hour ago her head had been pounding like it was about to split open. "Just get me up to speed."

Anna didn't look convinced but clicked the remote that switched on their TV. A camera feed came on-screen—the black-and-white, still image of the car that had run them off the road. "We backtracked your route and found the blue car you described at a stoplight six minutes before it caught up to you on the highway. Driver is a Caucasian male, forties maybe. It's hard to tell with the image so grainy."

"You can't clean it up, make it easier to make out?" Declan asked.

Portia shook her head. "Surveillance cameras are notoriously bad quality. A computer can't generate an image when there isn't enough detail there to formulate one from."

Lenny said, "Neither of you saw anything?"

Portia shook her head. "I woke up after the crash, and the gun was gone."

"As was the car that'd been following us," Declan said.

Portia turned to Anna. "License plate?"

"None that I saw."

"Just like the truck." This wasn't good. They needed leads, not a bunch of questions. Zero answers. Nothing but dead ends.

Anna nodded. "And it's an American brand of car. There are thousands of that model in that color registered in this county."

Portia chewed on her lip. "So we have nothing."

"What about the serial number on the gun?" Declan said.

She spun around to him while Anna said, "How would you get that?"

Portia said, "Of course."

She was going to blame forgetting that on the fact she'd hit her head. The temptation to touch the bandage, or adjust her hair made her fingers twitch. She was under no illusions that she wasn't just as fragile as any other human being on the planet, but that didn't mean she had to let her team know she was hurt.

Even until the end of his battle with cancer, her father had never done anything but be the strong man she'd known her whole life. The "how" of that end, she didn't want to think about.

She wandered to Anna's computer, where the agent was having Declan email her the notes he'd taken. "We'll get this run," Anna said. "See what information we get back."

"And if it's the same gun that was used to kill my father?"

"Tell me the make and model," Chris said, eyes on his computer. When the image popped up on Anna's screen she told him the make and model. The woman did know her guns. Chris said, "Not the same."

"Maybe it belongs to the truck owner and has nothing to do with any of this." Declan shrugged. "That's possible, right?"

Portia nodded. "Still, I think we were right in considering that gun a gift."

"One which someone considered important enough to run us off the road and steal," Declan said.

Anna folded her arms. "So one person wanted you to find it, and someone else took it from you?"

"It jibes with the theory we have one gunman and one sniper—separate suspects."

Declan shook his head. "Is this still one investigation?"

"It's certainly more complicated than premeditated murder and mistaken identity." And Portia didn't like that thought at all. The last thing she needed was for this to drag out and get more and more dangerous in the process. At some point she'd likely have to get Declan in a safe house just so she could make things less complicated. He wouldn't like it, but he would have to deal while she did her job. He was only an observer.

The man didn't have the jurisdiction to arrest anyone here. Even though he'd helped and been with her through crazy times since the first bullets had flown in the woods, she had to remember he wasn't an agent. He was only on the case because he'd thought his brother had been killed.

Portia couldn't get used to him. And she couldn't wind up in a place where she needed him.

That wasn't going to help her at all.

Portia's boss wandered over from her office. Portia got up from her chair and met the director in front of her desk.

The woman studied Portia with those knowing, dark brown eyes. Her gaze going particularly to the hair covering Portia's bandage. Did Director Golden know about the bump she'd received? The older woman looked at Declan. "Both of you are all right?"

Declan said, "Yes, ma'am. Thank you."

Portia filled her in on the details of the gun, particularly the fact Declan had noted the serial number.

"Copy me in when you get the results. Keep me apprised." She trailed away, to the next group of agents. Probably to get updated on their case.

Lenny sighed, leaning on the edge of his desk. "I don't like that we have no suspects right now. We need a lead that will narrow down our pool of people who might want to take a shot at Agent Stringer."

Declan's eyebrows rose.

Lenny said, "Just because people want to kill you doesn't mean you're not likable."

Portia nearly laughed at the two of them. Before she could, Anna said, "Uh-oh."

"What?" Portia moved to look at her computer screen.

"Squire just emailed me back." Anna put a case number into the database they used.

Portia's eyes widened at the results. "ATF?" She could imagine the federal agents whose jurisdiction was crimes related to alcohol, tobacco, firearms and explosives being all over illegal weapons sales.

"Ping."

She glanced at Declan. "The gun in the glove box might not be connected to the shooting in the woods, but it is connected. To an ATF case."

"Seriously?" Lenny said.

Even Chris had come over from his desk to get the scoop.

Anna said, "The gun was part of a group of weapons all decommissioned by the navy, headed for repurposing. Or destruction. Either way, they never got there."

"They were stolen?" Portia asked.

"Looks like it. The serial number Declan got us matched this case. It's one of the stolen guns, and ATF has been chasing them since the first one turned up in an illegal sale in Florida. They flagged the whole batch."

"Ping."

"Yep," Anna said.

Declan glanced between them. "What does that mean?"

Portia said, "It means our search just dinged on some ATF agent's computer. In a minute the phone is going to ring and they're going to want to know what we've got."

"Isn't that good? They could provide information, right?"

Portia shrugged and headed back to her desk. The last thing she wanted was a bunch of ATF agents showing up and getting in this investigation. It was already complicated enough.

Not to mention the likelihood that her ex-boyfriend was going to be among them. Steve worked locally. He was a team leader just like she was—or he had been two years ago when they parted ways. Portia had no desire to bring any of that up. Lenny and Anna—who'd been around back then as well—had barely quit rehashing that time in her life. Asking questions. Fishing for information about why she hadn't dated anyone since.

Certainly not because she had any lingering feelings for Steve.

She'd had to shut down the chatter because she didn't want Chris asking what they were talking about.

"Let's see what comes from it." Portia didn't want to think more about it. They needed information, and if it came from the ATF what difference did it make?

Just like everything else in her life, Portia was going to brace for the blow. Whatever it was, and however it came. She would weather it.

Declan pasted on a smile. "Well, I for one need more coffee."

Lenny glanced at him like he knew exactly what Declan was about. Not that it mattered. Portia shook her head. "I'm good."

"I'll give you a hand." Lenny moved toward the kitchen, not waiting for Declan to follow. The clock on the wall said three in the afternoon. Had he really been in Washington barely more than a day already? So much had happened since he'd landed yesterday morning. But that wasn't what was foremost in his mind right now.

He glanced once at Portia before he went. She had settled in her chair, still with that look on her face. She hid it well, but she expected the worst. Portia was the kind of person who assumed the other shoe would eventually drop.

Declan hadn't ever considered himself an optimistic kind of person. Compared to her, he was practically happy-go-lucky. Even with his sordid family history Portia beat him out anytime. She'd been worn down and battered by life over and over again. He could see it in her. No one kept their private turmoil to themselves the way she did. Not without having a very good reason for it.

Declan crossed the break room and leaned against the counter, the weight of all that had happened the last few days heavy on his shoulders. Lenny had answered a phone call on his cell, holding the phone between his shoulder and cheek while he made a fresh pot of coffee.

Did he want to know what was up with Portia? Part of him argued against what was essentially prying. Soon enough he'd be flying back to DC. And even if he eventually decided to make a career move away from the Secret Service, it wasn't necessarily going to be in this part of the country. The likelihood that Portia would be in his life long-term was slim. Even as much as he was coming to enjoy being around her.

Sure, it hadn't been much more than bullets flying, and the frustrations of him imposing on her case, but she was the kind of woman who…intrigued him. Yes, he was attracted to her. She was a beautiful woman, but she was also strong. Independent. Intelligent. Only a certain kind of man could balance out a woman like her.

The part of him that wasn't opposed to prying in her life wanted to know what it would be like to be that man. Soft when she needed it, unmoving when she needed to be held up. Steady. Partners, the way marriage was supposed to be. Declan had never considered himself the romantic type before. Maybe he'd simply never met anyone like Portia before. It was as though dormant parts of him were waking up for the first time. It was both intriguing and slightly uncomfortable.

Lenny glanced over, a curious look on his face as he studied Declan and listened to whoever was on the other end of his call at the same time. "Thank you. I'll make sure to give her that tonight before bed." He hung up.

Declan waited, leaving a space in case Lenny decided to chat about what the call had been.

Lenny turned back to the coffee, his straight jet-black hair settling on his forehead as he did so. "My mother has a nurse with her while I'm at work."

When he said nothing else, Declan asked, "And you take care of her when you're not? That must take a lot of your energy." Probably all of it, but Declan didn't know enough about that kind of thing to assume. It likely took all of Lenny's time off as well, effectively killing his ability to have a personal life.

"She was a wonderful mother to me, despite what my sister might think. It's my honor to take care of her when she needs it." He glanced over at Declan for a second, something like a shadow in his eyes. "It won't be long."

"I'm sorry."

Lenny shook his head. "It will be good for her, when the pain has finally passed. Like I said, she was a wonderful mother."

Declan nodded, not sure what to say. He got milk and the creamer from the fridge and handed them over.

"But you didn't want to know about my mother. You'd rather hear about Portia and the ATF agent who asked her to marry him."

Declan's mouth hung open. "I—"

Lenny laughed. "I know, you didn't ask. Nor did you particularly want to know *that*. But it is what it is."

"Her private life…"

"It's none of your business?"

"Well it isn't." He couldn't argue otherwise, despite curiosity. And that nagging attraction. "Who she…used to date really isn't any of my business."

Lenny eyed him. "It lasted nine months. Ended amicably enough if you consider the fact he didn't want to let her go. You have to give the guy credit for not letting her just drop him and walk away."

"She'd do that?"

"He got to her. Why else would she end it except because she's scared? Things got too real."

"Real isn't her thing?"

Lenny folded his arms. "Portia is my boss, and I don't really know you. But I'm going to go with my gut and tell you this as simply as possible, and then we're never going to speak of it again."

Declan waited.

"The right man is going to bring something out in Portia no one else has ever been able to dig up. It's going to be so worth it that the guy will never ever for the rest of his life forget what he has. There's not one chance anyone would take that for granted." Lenny paused. "Unfortunately, in doing so, it's not going to be pretty. She's going to fight tooth and nail giving up her freedom. Her independence. She's stubborn. So stubborn you're not going to believe it when you realize how deep that goes."

Lenny went on. "Did she hit her head in the crash?"

Declan nodded. "EMTs took care of it. No concussion."

"I thought so," he said. "And that's exactly what I mean. Keeping it to herself."

"Self-preservation?"

"It's easier to be in pain alone. No one needs anything from you, and no one expects anything of you."

Movement by the door caught his attention. He started to turn. "I know what that's—" He choked on the rest of what he'd been about to say. "Portia."

Her fiery gaze was firmly squared on Lenny. And if she could've produced some kind of laser ray from her eyes, she'd have burned her colleague where he stood. "Do we need to have words, Agent Chen?"

To the man's credit, he stood his ground. Lifted one of the cups. "Coffee?"

"Agent—"

Lenny lifted more mugs, juggling two in one hold and one in his other. "I'll just take these." He left two full coffees on the counter and strode past Portia out to the desks and the rest of the team. Both Anna and Chris were watching what was happening in the break room with avid interest.

Declan winced. "How much did you hear?"

"Enough to know my agent was spouting a bunch of mumbo jumbo about my personal life."

"He cares about you."

She didn't even respond to that. Instead, she said, "Anna has a list of everyone your father swindled. We need you to look at the pictures and see if you recognize anyone."

NINE

The ATF agent stood beside Anna's desk. Portia met his gaze, trying to decide whether she was disappointed or not that Steve hadn't been the one to come. It had been two years. She couldn't precisely say whether she wanted to see him or not. What she wanted was to finish this case so she and Declan could go somewhere they wouldn't wind up being shot at. Or chased.

Like to dinner. Because she was hungry.

The ATF guy nodded. "Agent Finch."

She nodded back. "Agent Mason didn't come with you?" The question left her mouth before she even realized. The tone had an edge of antagonism. Did she really think he'd chicken out coming here, and avoid her? He hadn't been like that. And this was a case of his.

"I'm over here." Steve walked toward her from the director's office. His smile was polite, but nothing more than that. Giving away no indication there had been anything between them. "How are you?"

"Good." She squared her shoulders, despite the fact her emotions were roiling. She could blame that on getting hit on the head. She might not have a concussion, and it didn't hurt as bad as it had, but still she wasn't at the top of her game.

Not that any of them would know that.

Declan's shoulder touched hers. Side by side. He stuck his hand out. "Agent Stringer. Secret Service."

Steve's eyebrows rose. "Mason." He shook Declan's hand. "ATF."

"We appreciate your help on this."

Steve looked aside at her. "We?"

Portia said, "The Secret Service is observing on this case." She wasn't going to tell an ATF agent about the mistaken identity of their murder victim, or that Declan came all the way from Washington, DC, because of it.

Presenting a united front felt good, even if she and Declan didn't know each other that well. They'd been through plenty together, yesterday and today. She wanted more time to just sit with him and talk. The man was easy to converse with and expected little from her. He was content to just let her be who she was, like that was a good thing. It was refreshing to be able to just…be.

She said, "Let's go in the conference room, and you can run down your case for us."

Portia led the way, though they all knew where it was. The director came in and sat at the head of the table. Declan took a seat beside Portia, with Steve and his colleague from the ATF across the table. Lenny, Anna and Chris sat, tablets in front of them.

Steve said, "We were talking about bringing this to NCIS soon anyway. It's interesting timing, considering when you ran the search on the serial number of that gun you found."

The director leaned back in her chair. "NCIS is more than happy to lend expertise if it will help."

"Nine months ago during a sting operation, we discovered weapons in a cache we hadn't been expecting. They were tacked onto the sale at the last minute, a new purchase the seller was trying to pass on to our buyer—an undercover agent. We brought down the seller, but since then he hasn't been forthcoming about these additional weapons and where they came from."

Portia didn't know if this would end up relating to her murder investigation, or to someone attempting to kill Declan out of revenge for his father's swindling. Still, it was interesting that they'd come across the gun in the course of their own case. Frank Parsons might have been involved in illegal weapons sales, but that didn't mean the killer was. The gun was in the dead man's truck, but the two things could be unrelated.

Steve continued, "Several of the weapons we've come across were navy. The one you guys found, specifically, was part of a batch of navy pistols, rifles and ammo being phased out. They were headed for decommissioning, designated old, broken or faulty. We've found several so far, all from that batch. Some using parts from different guns." He looked at Portia. "The weapon you found was the fifth."

"So they were stolen out of that shipment and sold on the black market?"

He nodded. "We think whoever did it takes a few at a time, then passes them on to contacts in exchange for cash. That way they fly under the radar."

"So you don't have an identity yet?"

"We looked into the personnel who moved the guns, admin staff for the paperwork and the driver who took the weapons to the facility where they're destroyed. So far no one has stuck out to us as being behind illegal sales."

So they had no leads? No wonder the ATF was here asking for information. If they were going to figure this out, they'd need all they could get from NCIS.

She thought for a second. "Did the weapons come from this base?"

"Yes."

"So this is a local deal," Portia said. "Like the murder."

"You think they're linked?" the director asked her.

"They very well could be, but until we have evidence I won't be able to say for sure." She looked at Steve. "Anything at all you can tell us about who is behind these sales?"

"Only a name. His handle on the dark web," Steve said. "Night-Chief."

That wasn't going to be a help. Unless… "Chris…?"

He was already out of his seat. "I'll get with Squire on the name." He left the room, and Portia's gaze snagged on Anna. The woman glanced at Declan, then at Steve. She widened her eyes and then looked down and tapped on her tablet screen. Portia's phone buzzed in her pocket. Whatever message Anna had just sent her—probably about Steve—Portia was going to ignore it. Her head had started to pound again. Besides, they could talk freely later. Now wasn't the time for that discussion. Even silently.

Steve pushed a flash drive across the table. "This is everything we have."

Portia nodded. Before she could grab the drive, Steve said, "We'd like your case file in return, so we can assess whether or not your murder is related."

"If it is, I'll let you know." She stood, snatching up the drive before he could change his mind.

Steve followed her to the hallway. "Portia."

She turned back. "I don't have to give you information about a murder case that has nothing to do with stolen weapons."

"Unless it does."

"Like I said, I'll let you know." She paused. "But this is my murder case, and I don't need help—"

"That sounds familiar."

"My team has got this."

"And a Secret Service agent."

Portia lifted her palms and let her hands drop back to her sides. "It is what it is."

"Funny, I don't remember you being great at sharing."

"Steve..." She didn't even know what to say. This wasn't a conversation they needed to have. Not when she had work to do and a headache to shake. "Thanks for coming over—I know you didn't have to make the trip yourself. You could have just emailed the information."

"Yes, I could have."

"So why did you come?" She was wary even in asking that question.

"Because I didn't want you to hear from someone else what I wanted to tell you."

"We've been broken up nearly two years. You don't owe me anything."

"No, but you move notoriously slow in every life decision you make. Two years to you is like six months of life for everyone else."

Portia shut her mouth, just so she didn't say something she'd regret. How was she supposed to respond to that, anyway?

"I'm getting married."

"He's getting married."

Declan glanced at Anna. "What was that?"

"My cousin works for DOJ." Anna leaned across the table, like she had a delicious secret to share. "She told me there's a gal in accounting in her office who started dating Steve about four months ago. My cousin told me they sent a card around in the office that said 'congratulations on your engagement.' I wasn't sure if I should tell Portia, or not. If she finds out I could've given her a heads-up and I let her get blindsided she isn't going to be happy."

"Is she going to be mad?"

"Maybe disappointed." Anna's freckled nose wrinkled. "She's my friend, as well as the senior agent on the team. I don't want to let her down."

"I have friends like that," he said. "It's hard to find people you can truly respect. But those are the friendships I have that lasted."

"You know, you're all right, Mr. Secret Service." Anna got up. "Do you want to come and look at those photos now?"

He nodded. They had gotten sidetracked by the arrival of the two ATF agents—the remainder of whom was seated at the other end of the table, staring at Anna in a way Declan didn't much like. Kind of like the way he reacted when other kids had picked on his brother at school. There wasn't anything bad about the look. Declan figured the guy was interested in her—maybe even attracted. But Declan wasn't going to let her be put on the spot if it would make her uncomfortable.

Declan sat at Anna's desk and looked through the photos while Anna and Lenny—who had also come back to his desk—talked through the case with Chris. When his eyes started to cross from the volume of pictures of strangers, Declan scrubbed his hands down his face.

Lenny said, "That's what's bothering me about this whole case."

"What's that?" Declan asked.

Lenny leaned on the edge of his desk. "Frank Parsons

is dead. Killed by someone in possession of the same gun used to kill your father."

Declan nodded. "Right."

"And now ATF says this other gun is linked to stolen weapons. But we don't know if it belongs to Frank, or the killer, right?"

Anna said, "So one, or neither of them, are connected to the ATF case."

Chris said, "So the gunman in the woods who shot at y'all could be part of the ATF case. Or the reason he met with Frank Parsons in the first place could be *because* of the illegal weapons sales."

Declan thought for a second. "If someone who wanted me dead heard Nicholas's name, even though it was a fake ID, maybe he made the meet to buy the weapon in order to kill him for personal reasons. Like a ruse."

"It's a long shot," Lenny said. "It links the two cases, and maybe the killer just thought he had a one-in-a-million chance to get revenge on the son of the man who ruined his life… Maybe he didn't check too much into the name, so he didn't know it wasn't the right Nicholas Stringer."

"He had to have known about the name change at least," Declan said, referring to his birth name versus the name he had now—his aunt's last name. "So he knew enough to know what our last name is now, but not enough to know the ID was faked? Seems sloppy."

Anna's mouth twisted to one side. "Or he's going to kill every Nicholas and Declan Stringer he comes across, just to be sure."

Declan shook his head. "That's crazy." He didn't want to think about this being a potential serial killer.

"What about the sniper?" Lenny asked. "He didn't manage to hurt either of you, though the tech got caught in the crossfire. So, was it a warning? You *were* in Frank

Parsons's apartment. Maybe there was something there to find."

Anna said, "Right. If Parsons was part of the illegal weapons sales, maybe there's something in his apartment that his cohorts don't want us getting our hands on."

"Wouldn't the technicians have found it?"

She shrugged. "Depends how well it was hidden."

Lenny said, "Might be worth another look."

"My head is spinning with all of this," Declan said. He couldn't help smiling, feeling out of his depth with this whole case. Why did Secret Service work seem almost simple compared to this?

Probably because he knew the ins and outs of it. Which was why the job had grown…almost stale in the last few months. Since his best friend transferred to San Diego. He just needed a shake-up, but a murder investigation—not to mention being shot at—wasn't the answer.

Declan scratched his jaw. "So we think the man in the woods is after me and Nicholas for personal reasons, and the sniper is part of the ATF case?"

Anna nodded. "I'd say that's a solid theory."

"Which means we're guessing."

"Until we have evidence, we can't say for sure," Lenny said. "That's why we need proof."

"Why does this feel like that carnival game where the thing pops up and you have to try and whack it before it hides again?"

Anna laughed. "That's about right." She patted his shoulder, then something beyond him caught her attention.

Declan turned in time to see Portia approach, a questioning look on her face as she glanced between Declan and Anna.

Lenny said, "We came up with an operation we believe might yield results. Or at least a lead."

"Okay, then."

Thirty minutes later Declan was sitting in the front passenger seat of Portia's car, beside her, down the street from Frank Parsons's apartment. Anna and Chris were parked farther down the street, beyond the residence. So they could see anyone approaching from that side.

"Thanks for sitting in on this."

Declan nodded, his attention on the apartment. "It beats sitting alone in my hotel room."

He heard a soft huff of laughter. "Maybe so, but it meant Lenny could stop in at home and check on his mom."

He knew there was a nurse involved, but said, "How bad is it?"

"They gave her weeks. Maybe less."

Declan pushed out a breath. "That's hard. My aunt had breast cancer when I was a teen. Went through surgery and treatments. It's not an easy thing, but I remember her saying she'd rather it was her than any of us. My uncle did not agree with her."

"And now?"

"I haven't spoken to her for a while. She ran a marathon last year, does a lot of fund-raising for survivors."

"That's great."

He smiled to the window. "My uncle wants her to slow down, maybe take a vacation, so she signed up for a triathlon in Hawaii."

Portia chuckled. "How old is she?"

"She'll be fifty-eight soon." He shook his head. "I can't believe it. They've been married thirty-two years this year."

"Wow."

"I know."

"And they're still happy?"

Declan laughed. "They're still friends. I think that helps, because if you can't get along, or relate to each other, then what are you supposed to talk about, you know?"

"I guess."

He glanced at her, saw that her attention was on the apartment. But she was frowning. "You don't think so?"

"Can't say I've ever thought about it." She shrugged one shoulder. "I've never been good at relationships. Just ask Steve."

Declan studied her.

"Anyway, thanks for coming." She shot him a small smile he didn't believe. "Not just for Lenny."

Declan had to wonder if she just wanted him there so she didn't feel alone over that lost relationship.

"Steve felt the need to tell me he was getting married," she said. "Why, I have no idea. That was two years ago. Maybe there should be more feeling there, maybe I should be sad or something. But I'm not." She glanced over. "Is that wrong?"

"You're entitled to feel whatever you feel. Can anyone say that's wrong, or not?"

"Maybe." She was quiet for a second.

Declan looked at the apartment.

"I told him 'Congratulations.' And you know what? I actually meant it. I'm happy he's getting married."

"What about you?"

"I'm not getting married."

Declan laughed. "Right now, or ever?"

"I guess I have to find the right person, don't I? This job doesn't leave a lot of time for personal relationships. After Steve and I broke up, I didn't make it a priority."

"So you haven't been looking?"

"I always just figured that if the right person came along, I'd know. That way it's special, and I know I'm not just making something of a relationship—pushing it where it shouldn't be taken—and it won't last."

Declan nodded. "I can see that."

"Instead, no one came along." Her voice was quiet, her head turned so she looked out the window. Away from him. "So I figured it was me. After that, I just...kept on with work. It was easy to make that the most important thing in my life. To ignore the fact I was lonely."

"I know what you mean."

And she'd said "*was* lonely." Did that mean she wasn't lonely now?

He bit the inside of his cheek to keep from asking her a question she probably wasn't ready for and caught movement along the sidewalk. "Hey, check this out."

Portia saw it, got on the radio and told Anna and Chris they would approach. She cracked her door. "Stay with me this time."

A man was headed for the apartment.

TEN

The man wore a uniform. Navy, a petty officer. Portia held her gun in a loose grip, low in front of her as she walked to the building and leaned her back against the stucco. He was upstairs now.

She moved to go after him, Declan right behind her—backing her up—and went far enough that she could see the guy at the door. If he broke in, she could arrest him. Otherwise, they could only request he answer some questions.

Declan moved to follow her, but she held one finger up and watched. The petty officer crouched and flipped the doormat. He lifted a key and let himself in.

She waved for Declan. When the petty officer cleared the front door, leaving it ajar, she moved to it and stood to one side. Declan put his shoulder to the stucco on the other side. They listened.

"Frank," the petty officer called out. Portia heard his footsteps as he crossed from carpet to vinyl flooring. "You better not be passed out again. The staff sergeant wants you on deck tonight."

Portia pressed the pads of her fingers to the door and eased it open, praying it wouldn't squeak like it had last time they were here.

She saw the petty officer head back into the hallway where the bedrooms were.

"I drove all the way across town," he called out. "You better be here."

She waited a minute or two until he emerged from the back rooms, a disappointed look on his face. Too young to be their shooter. The sniper, maybe?

Portia knocked twice on the door as she crossed the threshold, her gun angled down. It wasn't exactly non-threatening, but she would be ready. Both if this man reacted badly to their presence, and if he didn't.

"NCIS." She didn't give the man a second to think. "I'm Special Agent Finch. This is Secret Service Agent Stringer."

The man's eyes widened.

She motioned to a vinyl-covered barstool. "Have a seat. You have a name?" Like this was just a friendly chat... with Declan covering the front door in case the man decided to bolt. He didn't have to tell her anything, and she didn't have a warrant to arrest him. The most she could do was ask questions and hope he answered.

The petty officer rolled his eyes, then slumped onto the stool. "Sebastian Mallory. Mal."

She nodded. "Mal. You work out of Bremerton?"

"Yes, ma'am." Polite, but laced with belligerence.

"Frank Parsons a friend of yours?"

He shrugged. "I guess I'm not the only one looking for him."

She stowed her gun, since Declan still had his out. It would serve to make her appear a little less threatening. "When was the last time you saw him?"

"Friday night."

The night he died. "Time?"

Mal said, "Late, I guess."

"Where was he going when you parted ways?"

"To meet someone."

The killer? Portia wasn't sure she was going to get a straight answer out of this guy. "Who?"

"A friend of his, I guess." Mal made a face. "How should I know?"

"Frank Parsons was found dead Saturday morning."

Mal sputtered and lifted halfway off the stool.

"Sit back down." Portia took a step toward him. "Want to tell me why he had a fake ID that said Nicholas Stringer on him when he died?"

Out the corner of her eye she saw Declan shift his stance. She couldn't assume Mal would figure out who he was. He might not even know what the real Nicholas looked like, let alone be able to pick out a resemblance between him and Declan.

Mal sighed. "I knew that would come back to bite us."

"Someone else's idea?"

"It was an easy score. We were on a training mission in California, had a free night. When all those dumb sailors were drunk, we took their wallets."

"How many?"

"Six. Eight maybe."

Portia figured he knew the exact number but didn't push it. For now. Still, she had to wonder why he was essentially admitting to criminal activity. Could she prove he was part of an identity theft ring? Or maybe he was throwing this information at her like a smokescreen so she didn't look at him for something else he wasn't about to admit to.

She said, "Why'd you need a bunch of IDs?"

"Why else? To buy stuff with their money." Mal huffed. "They beat us on exercise, so we figured we'd get back at them. Run up their credit cards with all kinds of crazy stuff."

"The ID Frank had on him said Nicholas Stringer, but it was Frank's photo." Portia waited while that sank in. "You didn't know that?"

"What Frank was into didn't have nothing to do with me." There was a flash of something in his eyes, but Portia couldn't pinpoint what it was.

She settled on saying, "So he *was* into something."

Mal was silent.

"Maybe it involved that 9 mil in the glove box of his truck."

Mal's eyes flashed. "I told him not to keep that thing."

"Because it was stolen, and traceable? Sounds to me like you're a whole lot smarter than Frank was."

Mal didn't react. He simply waited.

"Smart enough to tell me everything you know about stolen IDs, stolen weapons and exactly who Frank's friends are." She paused. "Starting with that staff sergeant you mentioned."

Mal's gaze narrowed.

She saw it coming, and said, "Don't." Then added, "You can talk to me or the ATF. It's your choice. But someone is going to hear everything you know." She had to push him, or she'd never get any answers. She hadn't seen any sign yet that he was injured—which meant he was likely not the shooter from the woods. But he could still have information.

A muscle in his jaw flexed. "I'm under arrest?"

She shook her head. "Come with me back to the NCIS office and we'll talk." Just a simple questioning, gathering information.

For now.

"Only if you say it's because I'm cooperating in an investigation. If it gets back to my commanding officer that I'm involved in something, I'll get in trouble."

"He doesn't have a problem with you guys stealing those wallets?"

Mal snorted. "It was his idea to get back at them."

Portia blinked. Her report on this to the director was going to be interesting—and would likely result in another case being opened. She couldn't help the truth getting out—or being written in a report and put in Sebastian Mallory's service record. That was between him and his commanding officer.

This accusation, that his C.O. had been behind the theft, would need to be followed up on.

Portia said, "If you want it known that you cooperated, then cooperate. That's the kind of special agent I am."

"And him?" Mal motioned toward Declan.

"He's from out of town. He's observing."

Mal shot him a questioning look. "Okay." He sighed. "I'll come in."

As they made their way to the car, Anna and Chris were walking up to the apartment. Portia motioned to the residence with a nod of her head, and Anna said, "Got it."

Satisfied they would let her know if they found anything inside, she drove Declan and Mal—who sat quietly in the backseat—to the office.

Mal probably wanted the drive time to think what he was going to say. To formulate what else he should let get out, and what he shouldn't. That didn't matter. They would look into his life and find out what he knew.

Anna and Chris—or the ATF—could visit his apartment next and see if there was anything there which linked him to all this. Squire would go through the man's phone records—try to figure out who he and Frank were linked to. Something would give them a lead that would pan out. She was sure of it.

Declan said, "You want me to fill in Steve?"

Portia nodded. "He'll want to be present for the chat."

While he typed on his phone, Portia ran through the details of the case so far. They needed a link between Frank and these illegal weapons dealers. One that led to the killer's identity. Would Mal tell them who this "friend" was, the one the dead man had been supposed to meet the night he was killed? It could be their killer, and it might not.

They had entirely too many loose ends, and not enough answers as to what was going on. What had started out as a revenge killing had turned a corner into illegal weapons sales. So which had come first? Or was this the proverbial chicken-and-egg scenario, and they would never get to the bottom of it all?

Maybe Mal knew nothing. And maybe he was the key to them breaking this case wide open.

Either way, Portia was going to find out.

Declan watched through the window as Portia interviewed the suspect. She'd successfully unpacked the man's entire life, working through his service record. Proving he had motive to be part of a group using decommissioned navy weapons, which should have been destroyed, to make money. The man was in debt in a way it would take him decades to clean it up. And yet for the last few months had been cash-flowing his lifestyle. Which seriously didn't correlate with his military income.

Mal hadn't been able to explain that.

Portia sat back in the chair, at ease. She was in command in the interview room, just as she had been holding her gun. Or chasing down that homeless man. And yet, she'd also been able to make Mal comfortable enough that he'd lost that initial anxiety and was now chatting. Just like she'd also done with the homeless man. Mal wasn't speaking freely—the man had more self-preservation than that—but he was giving up information.

Declan turned to Lenny. "Is she just that good at her job?"

"Portia has been doing this for a long time, but the way she is with interviewees..." Lenny shrugged. "She's a natural."

Declan turned to watch her listen to the petty officer. Now that he was here, they were working on putting together charges to be filed. Mal likely didn't want to go to jail for murder, when he would get a much lighter sentence on weapons sales. He needed to offer up whatever Portia wanted to know about his friend in order to get out from under suspicion of being involved.

Portia said, "We're going through your phone. If you're connected to this friend Frank was meeting, we'll know."

Mal kept his gaze on the table. Declan watched as his shoulders lowered. Portia was right. There was no sense in hiding anything from her. Not with forensics the way they were these days. Plus the fact most people broadcasted their entire lives on their phones and social media.

Connection came with a price, and that price was exposure. In Mal's case, it would incriminate him in a way that meant the ATF was about to be his worst nightmare. He would be their primary lead tracking down the people trafficking in weapons.

Declan could see his mouth twist. Mal shifted in his seat. "I said I didn't know who it was."

"See, here's the thing," Portia said. "I think Frank was going to meet a buyer. He was making a deal with someone, right? Selling one, or some, of the weapons you guys got from the shipment."

"No one missed it. Never even knew." Mal's eyes

gleamed, and Declan realized she'd gotten to him. She'd appealed to his pride.

"Took them right out from under the brass's noses. That it? Or was your C.O. in on it, like the theft?"

Mal shrugged. "No one missed them. Hardly my fault."

He wasn't going to answer the question? "It makes you complicit."

"Whatever. I was gonna get caught sometime. But you're not pinning that murder on me."

"And if I can prove you were, in fact, complicit in that?"

Mal sputtered.

"What if we find evidence on your phone that the meet was your idea? That this 'friend' was a buyer, and you sent Frank to do that deal."

"He *requested* Frank."

"Frank, or Nicholas Stringer?"

Declan's stomach knotted. Had the man been targeted all because they'd stolen the IDs of those marines in California? Nothing but coincidence had led to the death of Frank Parsons. Killed because of a driver's license in Nicholas Stringer's name?

If the killer had done enough homework to figure out that Declan and Nicholas had changed their names, why hadn't he known that Frank was not Nicholas? It seemed wrong that the killer had done so much work, only to fall down at the end…and kill the wrong person.

Mal blinked. "Does it matter?"

Portia shrugged. "It might. Depends."

"On what?"

"Tell me what the guy's name was."

It was the only way they would figure out who was targeting Declan and his brother. He hadn't been able to

ID any of the people his father had swindled money from. He'd been through the photos twice, but didn't recognize a single one. Neither had he seen any of them recently.

Declan clenched and unclenched his fingers. Why couldn't he help more? Yes, he was here to observe. But it was niggling at him not being able to take action. His pride was suffering a hit just sitting there, not being able to contribute in a meaningful way. Was that God growing him, teaching him to let go of his need to control everything? Lives were at stake, but did the Lord want him to learn something through all of this? The alternative was leaving here the same way he'd come, and Declan didn't like the idea of that at all.

Mal raised his voice. "I said I *don't know* who he was."

"How did you get in contact with him?"

"The classifieds." Mal shot her a look. "How do you think we sell illegal weapons?"

"In the newspaper?"

He shrugged. "Only people who read it are old guys with like, retirement money and stuff. They buy guns. Especially old ones. Collector's items. I should have one of those TV shows where they find old stuff in people's garages and fix it up. Sell it on. But with *guns*."

Beside him, Lenny snorted.

In the interview room, Portia was quiet for a minute. Declan figured she just didn't know what to say to this twentysomething navy serviceman and his insane idea that was also totally illegal.

The door to the interview room opened, and Steve entered.

Portia said, "Mr. Mallory, this is Steve Mason. Bureau of Alcohol, Tobacco, Firearms and Explosives."

Mal's eyebrows rose. "What are you..."

"He'll be taking care of things from here."

"You said—"

"You can't provide me anything of value that will help me solve this murder, and so all that's left for me to do is pass you over to ATF. They can take care of you now." Portia stood. "I'm sure they have some questions."

Mal continued to sputter as she left the room.

Declan exited the viewing room and met her in the hall.

Lenny stuck his head out of the viewing room. "Squire has something for you."

Portia nodded.

"Agent Stringer!"

Declan turned to see a security guard trot up the hall. "Yes."

"I've been looking for you. Got a report from the duty security guard patrolling the parking lot that someone was tinkering with your car a few minutes ago. We've put a call up the chain, and—"

Portia said, "Go check it out."

Declan nodded. He got instructions from the guard and made his way to where he'd parked. Nothing looked amiss now. A security golf cart was parked close to the car, and the guard sat in the driver's seat, on his radio.

When he saw Declan, he said, "Bomb detection dogs are on their way."

Declan nodded. It made the most sense that someone messing with his car had been planting a bomb. He scratched at his chin and took a step closer to the vehicle. It was dark, so he wouldn't be able to see wires. Not that he wanted to get close when he didn't have equipment, or even a flashlight. Finding explosives was what the dogs, and their handlers, did for a living.

He sighed and turned back to the guard…

The man was standing much too close. Then his arm

shifted and the gun came up, the barrel pointed right at Declan's chest.

Declan started to move, but the shot blasted right at him. Before he could do anything, the shot hit him, square in the chest. Air expelled from his lungs in a rush as he fell backward.

Hit the concrete. There was so much pain.

Everything went black.

ELEVEN

Portia pushed open the door to Forensics and sent the text asking Declan if his car was okay. Squire said, “Ah, you’re here. Good.”

“What do you have?” For whatever reason she couldn’t explain, Portia wanted to make sure Declan was all right. Base security was with him, but it wasn’t good that someone had been snooping around his rental car.

At least he hadn’t driven it. She didn’t want to think about an explosion. Declan caught in it. No, that didn’t bear thinking about. And not because she was getting used to him shadowing her. Just concern for a colleague, that was all.

Working together over the last few days had reminded her what it was like to have a partner. In work, and, yeah, in life, as well. To an extent. She enjoyed being in the car with someone else instead of alone. She enjoyed sharing meals with a professional who worked on the front lines of this country, as she did. They both endeavored to make people safe. To make sure that huge infrastructure kept on chugging along—her, the military, and him, the presidency.

Everything she was learning about Declan made her confident that whoever sat at the desk in the Oval Office would be protected.

Squire said, "I scoured Mallory's phone for any details about Frank Parsons and the man he was meeting with, hoping to get an identity on our gunman."

"And?" She wouldn't be here if he hadn't found something substantial that would be relevant to the case. Still, she was surprised he'd found so much this quickly. Though, it was Squire. Maybe she shouldn't be *that* surprised.

He grinned. "I traced the conversation thread where he set up the meeting and got the original introduction. Sounds like there's an interested third party also selling weapons."

So there was history between the killer and the victim before his death. History that would be documented as evidence, and which would assist in their case.

Portia thought. "If he was after Nicholas Stringer, then the weapons sales could've just been a front. A way to draw him in with a promise of business," she mused aloud. Still part of the ATF case, whichever way she looked at it. Yet the personal connection to Declan couldn't be denied. Two Stringer brothers associated with a case—and shot at, one "killed"—couldn't be a coincidence. "Any idea on his identity?"

If they could figure out who the gunman was, they could put out a notice to local police, FBI and the rest of NCIS. Get everyone looking for him before he hurt someone else.

Squire clicked a few keys and a man's DMV record came on-screen. In his fifties, the man had a scruffy beard threaded with gray that matched his salt-and-pepper hair. "Meet Benjamin Mercer."

That was some seriously good work. "Squire..."

"There's more." And judging by the man's facial expression, it wasn't good.

"It took some digging, but Benjamin Mercer is the name of one of the stolen IDs Mallory and his friends took in California."

Portia felt her eyebrows rise. "So Mallory knows him, or one of his friends does. Enough that he got this ID."

They could be strangers, but that was far too much of a stretch. Stealing fake IDs for personal use, Mallory had said. Not so they could be sold on. Their gunman had been part of Mallory's group who all received fake IDs. How many were there?

Squire nodded. "Real name, Bill Frawley." He clicked more keys, and another—expired—DMV record popped up. "This ID has gone dark at this point. He's basically living as Benjamin Mercer right now as far as I can tell. Credit cards show a motel for a few nights a week ago, then cash taken out of an ATM. Take-out charges for food."

If they could only find out where he was staying now. Then they would be able to snatch him up. Portia both loved and loathed this point of the case. When the killer was so close, and yet still just out of reach.

"Bill Frawley has a military service record. Marines, dishonorably discharged. His brother Eric Frawley served as a sniper. Also dishonorably discharged. It was the same incident, over ten years ago now."

That explained his age in the photo, and the graying hair. Not that there weren't older marines, especially among the career crowd. "Either of them could be the man I saw in the forest. Did the discharge have to do with selling weapons illegally?"

"That wasn't the whole of it. I've sent the file to Anna already, so she'll fill you in, but there were suspicions noted. Neither of them went to jail, though. No evidence. No charges brought against them."

Two men. Military careers—one a sniper. It explained a lot about the two gunmen they'd faced. Declan and Portia were extremely fortunate to have gotten this far unscathed. "What are they up to now?"

"Good question," Squire said. "The brother is dark. No ID. Totally off-grid. I'm finding snatches of info on Bill, including blogs linked to an activist group. I'm looking into it, but it's not much."

"Keep working on it. See what you come up with."

He nodded, distracted. Focused on his monitor screen. "There it is."

She looked at the information he seemed to think gave him something but couldn't see what he did. "What is it?"

"The connection. Bill and Eric Frawley's father." Squire turned to her, a dark look on his face. "His name is on the list of people Declan's father swindled. Invested his entire life savings and all his retirement money with the Ponzi scheme. He lost everything."

Portia blew out a breath. "So this whole thing *is* personal." She pulled out her phone and called Declan. When he didn't answer, she left him a message asking him to call her when he was done with Security.

His life was in danger from these two former marines. Men with the skills and means to fulfill their personal mission. The sooner he was where she knew he would be safe—and yeah, where she could keep an eye on him—the sooner she would feel a whole lot better.

Portia shook her head slowly. "So they heard the name Nicholas Stringer somehow. Didn't know it was one of the fake IDs, like the one Bill was using. They killed Frank because he was using the name Nicholas Stringer. Then when Declan showed up they tried to kill him, as well."

It made the most sense. More than any other theory she'd heard so far as to why the killer had stuck around to shoot at Declan. And why it had seemed as though there was more than one gunman.

"All because their father lost his money," Squire said. "Then killed himself." He motioned to a newspaper report. "Eric, the sniper and the older of the two brothers, was in the Marines by then. Bill hadn't graduated from high school yet."

"So when Declan's father was jailed, they were old enough to know exactly what was happening." Old enough to hate the offspring of the man who had ruined their lives. She said, "That's good work."

Squire's phone rang. He snapped it up with one hand, attention still on the monitor screen as he said a distracted "Forensics." He blinked and turned to her. "I'll tell her." Squire hung up. He opened his mouth but said nothing.

"What?"

"Declan was shot in the parking lot."

"That was a perfectly good shirt you just cut up." Declan eyed the EMT with the scissors. This guy better not come at him again with those things. He shifted on the stretcher in the ambulance and pulled the Velcro tabs on his vest.

"Good thing you had that on."

Declan gritted his teeth. The bullet was still embedded in the front of the vest he'd been wearing under his shirt. He lifted the hefty white material over his head so that he was only in his undershirt, pants and shoes.

"It's so thin," the EMT said, eying the vest.

"Secret Service issue. Has to go under our shirts without making it look obvious we're wearing protective vests." He paused in talking to pull in a breath through pursed lips. The EMT didn't need to know how much it hurt. He lifted his undershirt.

"Ouch." The guy eyed the bruise on Declan's sternum. It hurt to even think about breathing. "You probably cracked something."

Declan gritted his teeth.

"I'll take you in. You need an X-ray."

He shook his head. Bad idea. Even that movement made him want to hurl. Moving enough to get his button-down shirt back on didn't help.

"Seriously? You're just going to go with the tough-guy routine?"

Declan reached the end of the bed and glanced back with just his head moving, not his shoulders or torso. He kept his body straight. Passing out wouldn't look good. "The attitude is standard-issue. Like the vest."

The EMT shook his head. Declan ignored the man's look and climbed out of the ambulance. Slowly, so he didn't pass out. Every time he breathed it felt like knives in the spot where that guy had shot him. Point-blank range.

He should be dead.

He wasn't.

Two navy cops he'd seen in Portia's office had shown up. Declan had put them off while the EMT fussed over him, and now one was heading over.

"Agent Stringer."

Declan nodded. "I didn't see his face."

"We're pulling the feeds from Security to see if we can get an ID. My partner went to check with base Security so we can get to the bottom of how he got in, managed to pose as a security guard and then called up to the office. All in an effort to draw you out." The agent paused. "Sure you don't want to see a doctor?"

Declan needed to wrap the bruise on his sternum, just to take the pressure off. That was all. "I'm good."

The guy didn't look impressed.

"Declan!"

He turned too fast and sucked in a breath. Placed his hand on top of the bruise. "Portia." He tried to smile, but his heart wasn't really in it.

The agent standing by him muttered, "Sure you're okay."

Declan ignored that. Portia joined their huddle. She moved awkwardly, like she didn't know whether to just stand there, or shake his hand. *Congratulations, you're still alive.* Or maybe even hug him. He'd take a good hug right now. Even if it would make him pass out.

"Are you okay? They said you were shot."

Declan nodded, not yet sick of that question. Not when it was coupled with a whole lot of compassion. Portia actually cared. It was so surprising to see that he couldn't think what to say for a second. The first thing that came out was, "Worried about me?" Like a total moron, smiling at the idea of her being worried about him.

The other agent thankfully made a strategic exit. Probably thinking Declan was an idiot—which he kind of was. The compassion that had been on Portia's face was gone now, and she was frowning.

"They said you were *shot.*"

Declan swallowed. "Sorry. I was." He touched his chest. "Saved by the vest, I guess."

She shook her head. "Next time you go somewhere, you don't go alone." She filled him in on the two former marines, brothers, one a sniper.

"Our two shooters?" His head spun with this new information.

She nodded, studying him. "Don't worry. We'll find them."

"I know you will."

Declan didn't exactly want or need a shadow to protect him in the meantime. Still, having two men after him made him want to consider it. Having someone at his back was never a bad plan. It was why they worked in teams at the Secret Service, and not as solo operators. Even though Portia was the one who'd reminded him of that fact, using it to plead her case.

Here, in Washington State, he was at the mercy of NCIS and their dictates. Portia could override his desire to remain in control of his own situation. She could legitimately decide he should be in a safe house—and there would be little Declan could do about it when she had logic on her side.

Is that what she would do?

Declan said, "Don't shut me out of this, keeping me holed up somewhere."

"You want to work this case?" Portia asked. "I thought that's what we *were* doing, and you got shot this time."

"Portia—"

"You're completely pale. Did you know that?" She set her hands on her hips. "You look like you're going to pass out."

"A chair would be good."

She walked with him to her office building, and they went up the elevator to her floor. At her desk, Portia waved him to her chair and thankfully turned away. While she went to the monitors to study the new information they had about the brothers, Declan sat. The world spun, and he made a point to breathe through his nose. When he opened his eyes, Anna was staring at him.

"Nine mil?"

Declan nodded.

"Broken sternum?"

"Feels like it."

Anna blew out a breath. "Happened to me once. Hurt like you *would not believe*."

Declan smiled. He couldn't help it. Anna just had the ability to put a person at ease—when she wasn't pointing a weapon at them. He was glad he wasn't one of her suspects. And he could see why Portia seemed to like working with Anna, Lenny and Chris. He didn't know them well, but they were good people.

They made him miss his friend and fellow Secret Service agent, Grady Farrow. Now there was good people—Grady and his fiancée. Since Grady had taken a post in San Diego, Declan had been feeling more and more like Washington, DC, was missing something. Maybe just his friend. And he could admit to himself that he might need a new challenge somewhere else, as well.

But not because of a woman. And not here, where he'd been shot at. But if there were good people like this elsewhere, then he could handle the change. Find a new life. Build something for himself, the way Grady was doing with Skylar in California.

Portia turned. "Agent Sparrow, do you have anything new to add that is relevant to this case?"

"Actually, I might." Anna clicked keys while Portia walked over. Declan didn't think she was mad that Anna hadn't been working, but instead had been chatting with him. She didn't seem like that kind of boss. He wondered if she might be mad for another reason—like the fact he'd been shot. Or she didn't want to be reminded of that or Anna's evidently having gone through a similar thing.

Declan opened his eyes, realizing he'd been drifting.

"I can go without you, if you want to stay here and rest." Portia's gaze softened on him.

"I'm awake." He looked at his watch. It was that late? "We're going tonight?"

She stared at him for a while, then sighed. "First thing tomorrow. And I don't want you leaving without protection, so you bunk on the couch in the break room. You aren't alone until we find these brothers."

Declan found he was too tired to argue with her. "Okay. Deal." He pushed out a breath, trying to find some energy reserves. "What did Anna find?"

"An address for Bill Frawley's daughter." Portia's eyes gleamed. "We're going to find out if she knows where her father is."

TWELVE

Portia sipped from the paper cup of her favorite drive-through coffee place. Not the one everyone else frequented. And not one of those hipster places that used words like *infused* and *undertones*. Whatever that meant. She just wanted espresso and milk, not something completely overcomplicated.

She'd been up late last night arranging for local cops to watch Bill's daughter's house to make sure she didn't leave. And to see if her father stopped by. But he hadn't shown up, and the cops reported that she'd gone to bed around ten and woken up a short time ago. They'd also told Portia she worked at a grocery store and had today off.

Portia glanced at Declan for a second, then focused on the freeway. He didn't need to know that she'd really only stayed at the office last night to make sure he was okay. Yes, there was no way a gunman would've come all the way to the break room to shoot him, but she wouldn't have said one could pose as base security either. And yet, he'd been shot exactly that way.

It wasn't more than a three-hour drive to Portland, where Bill Frawley's daughter lived—provided traffic was going to cooperate. Which it usually didn't. Still, there were only a few minutes left of travel time. Declan's soft snore had been sweet for a while. Then she'd turned on talk radio and listened to their overly emotional chattering.

She glanced at him again, and then changed lanes.

His lips moved. "I can feel you staring."

The corners of her lips curled up and she looked back at the freeway. "Sorry."

"I thought you didn't mind being alone."

"I'm not alone. You're here, aren't you?" He had been sleeping. Now, as they were closing in on the outskirts of Portland, he had apparently awakened without her even being able to tell.

"True." He lifted his head from the bundled jacket he'd shoved against the window and set the jacket on his lap. "But you do kind of seem like the Lone Ranger type."

Maybe that had been true for a while. Something about Declan being here made her want to…be with him. To talk. Maybe share things she didn't normally share with others.

"My dad and I were a team. For years. Two-peas-in-a-pod, all his friends said. We'd go camping, fishing, hiking. Every weekend we'd pack up the truck and just drive. Take the boat out on some lake, or on the ocean, and just…get lost together."

She pulled in a breath, not looking at Declan but feeling his attention on her. "When he deployed I'd go stay with an elderly neighbor. On the weekends I'd sneak back home and sleep in my dad's bed. He would call me on the home phone." She smiled at the memory of that old rotary-dial phone. "He knew I'd be there."

"I can see you as an independent kid. The kind who doesn't need anyone's help. You probably packed your own lunches and did your own laundry."

Portia shrugged. Didn't every kid do that stuff?

"Being self-sufficient isn't a bad thing."

She swallowed down the rush of emotion, not wanting to talk about herself. Not even really wanting to talk about her father more than she already had. This was more than she'd spoken about him to anyone for years. "When he got sick he didn't even tell me. Not at first. It was when we were fishing one time. He just couldn't stop throwing up over the side of the boat. Six months later..."

"Portia." He reached for her hand and she realized she was holding the steering wheel in a death grip. She relaxed her hand and signaled for the next exit. Tears wet her cheeks. She swiped them away and found a parking lot. Some restaurant or store. She didn't know. Just parked in the first spot, not caring that she was completely crooked in the space.

She put the car in Park and covered her face with her hands.

"Hey." He rubbed across her shoulders with the warm palm of one hand. His long fingers massaged the knots in her shoulders. "I'm sorry you lost your father. It must have been devastating to have that hole in your life suddenly."

She realized then that he'd lost his own father, but that he'd never had anywhere near the close relationship with his dad that she'd had. She was being completely insensitive. Thinking only about her own loss and not taking his situation into consideration. She looked over at him. "I'm so sorry. I didn't think..."

Declan shook his head. "Don't apologize. You lost your dad. Don't worry about me."

"But—"

"I'm fine, Portia. I don't want you to be sad, but I do want to hear about your father."

"Some people say they're fine, and they mean anything *but* what they said."

"Steve?"

She shot him a look. "He isn't part of this. And he hasn't been in my life for a long time."

"Sorry. That wasn't called for."

"Seems like both of us should just call it good. Wipe the slate clean and start over."

A spark flared in his eyes. She didn't know what it was, or what it meant. But she did think it had to do with her. He said, "We can start over, as long as it's together."

She decided to lighten the mood, since the conversation was getting heavy. "Is your near-death experience messing with your head?"

"We don't joke about that."

Too soon, apparently.

"But you know what?" he said. "Yeah, maybe. I mean, I was shot. If he'd checked to see if I was dead, or if he'd shot me in the head, then I wouldn't be here."

His phone rang then, breaking whatever moment they'd been having. He frowned. "One second." He answered his call, keeping his attention on her.

Portia looked back at the road. Getting distracted by him wasn't going to help. That wasn't what they were here for. She had to remember that, to focus on the job.

And the fact Declan had insinuated himself into her investigation in the first place.

Whatever epiphany he'd had didn't have anything to do with her. That was for sure. No matter that she might—maybe—admit to being attracted to him, what did that matter? He wasn't staying, and she wasn't interested in a man who would just turn out to be exactly like every other man she knew.

Declan knocked on the front door. Anna had called ahead, strategically not mentioning the fact cops had been on the street all night and confirmed Bill Frawley's daughter was willing to speak with them. That was a start. He figured if it was him in her place he'd have chosen now to take a vacation, considering the alternative was to be drawn into an investigation.

It'd been hard enough being a kid with his dad getting arrested. All he'd had to deal with was questions and comments at school. He didn't want to know what it would be like to be an adult and face the fact a close relative was a criminal.

Beth Frawley opened the front door of her new-looking town house. The rent was probably exorbitant. But then, wasn't that happening everywhere these days?

Her gaze lifted as she took in Declan. "NCIS?"

He glanced at Portia. "This is Special Agent Portia Finch, NCIS. I'm Declan Stringer, Secret Service." They both flashed credentials at her.

"Oh..." Beth said, studying the badges. "Did my father threaten the president again?" Even while she asked, the young woman stepped back and opened the door all the way.

"Again?" If he'd done it before, Secret Service intelligence would have noted the threat. Serious enough threats warranted further action. To the point that if the president was coming to town, those who had made a threat would receive a visit from the advance team.

Portia followed her down the short hall to a living room with a slipcovered old couch and two beanbags. Toddler blocks and storybooks littered the floor and a sippy cup peeked out from under a frayed cushion.

Declan stayed by the TV while Beth and Portia took a seat. Beth brushed crumbs from the couch. "I just put Samuel down for his morning nap."

Portia smiled. "How old is he?"

"Eight months next week." Beth relaxed into the couch. "Light of my life."

"Has your father met Samuel?"

"Is that your subtle way of asking me if he's been here recently?"

Portia shrugged. She'd successfully put the woman at ease, and he didn't think that had backfired. Not completely.

"He's seen Samuel a couple of times," Beth said. "But I told him not to come anymore unless he's sober."

Portia nodded. "My father was an alcoholic, as well. He went to meetings, did that whole thing. He was dry nearly fifteen years before he died. But the damage still killed him."

The look in her eyes made Declan wonder what the whole story was. And if she would ever tell it to him. Portia seemed content to keep her own confidence, though she'd started to open up to him in the car.

A long-distance relationship wasn't what he wanted, but he couldn't deny he was attracted to her. He needed to shut that down before it got worse. Especially considering the fact it seemed like she didn't have anything but professional politeness to give him.

They weren't a team.

There couldn't be anything between them.

Portia said, "Do you have any idea where your father or your uncle Eric might be?"

"Eric is crazy. Who knows where he is?" Beth shook her head. "My father, I don't know either. I have a phone number for him. Is that all you need?"

Declan prayed that Bill could rein in Eric. Or at least help them to bring him in. He said, "It's possible that answering some questions could jog loose a memory, or an idea of where he might be." He pointed to a small picture frame on the mantel. The only personal memento in the room, it was an image of Beth as a teen standing alongside her father outside a cabin in a forest somewhere. "For example, places your father might have frequented."

"We rented that cabin every year for…years." She shrugged. "I don't even know if it's still standing. It was pretty dilapidated even back then."

Portia said, "It's enough that NCIS would like to check it out."

Beth said, "I know the general area, but I have no clue what the address is." She gave a vague location, which Portia noted on her phone.

"And anything else that you can think of might be a location your father would use as a stopping point?"

"Do you know about United American Citizens?"

Portia nodded. "We've come across them as part of the investigation. Namely, when we found the blogs your father had written. Is he still close with them?"

"I didn't think so, but it's poss—"

A baby cry cut off her words. The monitor on the coffee table flashed red, and the sound crackled through the speakers.

"Sorry." Beth stood. "You need to leave now."

Portia stood, as well. "Thank you for your time."

She shook both their hands, and they left with the paper Beth had written on. Over the roof of the car, Declan asked, "Do you think this will give us anything?"

"Maybe. Maybe not. I'll pass the information to Anna and Chris, and we'll just have to see what they come up with."

Declan nodded, and they climbed in. They were on a time crunch. "So, where to now? The office?"

Portia glanced at the dash clock. "If we can get out

of Portland before rush hour, we'll hit the office about lunchtime."

On that cue, Declan's stomach rumbled.

"Food first. Then work."

He nodded. "Great." Even though it didn't feel much like it was. They were at a stalemate unless she admitted she felt the same way about him as he did about her. Which he couldn't see happening.

Even wondering about that interested him more than any relationship in a long time. Why was that? What was it about Portia that just the idea of her in his life going forward sparked more in him than any woman he'd ever known?

He was probably delusional. Or he'd hit his head, or something. She didn't want a relationship with him.

Declan took a couple of painkillers, since the ache in his chest had started pounding again. Within a few minutes he'd drifted off.

He woke up when a car collided with the back of them. Again? Last time the gun had been stolen, and they'd been left with bruises.

Portia muttered under her breath, both hands gripping the wheel. "Hold on. Things are about to get bumpy."

She cut the steering wheel hard to the right. They careened over the rumble strip onto brush at the side of the road. Another bump, and they kept going.

Down a narrowing dirt track that dropped off to nowhere.

THIRTEEN

Portia gripped the wheel, thankful she was driving her own car. She shifted from Drive to third gear so the engine would do the braking for her, without her hitting the pedal. It would give her better traction, and hopefully keep them from careening out of control.

Off a cliff.

They were now half a mile off the highway, somewhere in southern Washington. Behind them the lights of a lifted 4X4 truck lit up the rearview mirror so that all she saw behind her was glare. Atop the roof of the truck, two more lights cut through the gloom of this cloudy day.

Too bad for the guy behind her, she'd been driving on roads like this since she was fourteen and her dad let her sit on a phone book so she could reach the pedals.

Declan shifted to look out the back window. "He's right on top of us."

He touched the spot on his chest where he'd been hit by that bullet and hissed out a breath. But Portia didn't have time to worry about him. She shifted back to Drive and hit the gas. Took the tight turn that wound in a hairpin.

The truck would struggle on some of these dirt tracks, the wheels wider than hers. But she couldn't count on the fact he'd misjudge some turn and go over the edge.

No, she had to get them out of this herself.

The truck engine roared. It bore down on them.

A gunshot rang out.

The back window shattered. Portia gripped the wheel and kept it steady as she turned. The road inclined downward. She shifted back to third again, and the engine changed gear. The car slowed. The truck drew closer.

If he hit her now, this would be the end. She had to fight between basic safety and not dying. One wrong move and…bye.

What if she couldn't do this? *God, I need Your help.* Praying didn't come naturally. Not when she could take care of herself. But Portia had to face the fact this was out of her control. Whatever she did, it might not be enough to keep them alive. Only God could save them.

They passed a driveway, the house completely still. No cars parked there. Blinds drawn. Portia drove on. This neighborhood in the middle of nowhere was likely a maze of streets that ensured anyone who didn't live there got completely lost.

The farther she drove, the lower the chance they were going to find the highway again. Headed back to Seattle, they'd been going north. Now they were headed northeast. She turned a bend. Southeast. Farther and farther from their destination.

She glanced at the dash screen. "Hit the phone button." She pointed for a second, then gripped the wheel again.

Declan understood enough that he got in her recent calls. He found the entry where Lenny had updated her on everything while Declan had been sleeping. He tapped it and the car, connected by Bluetooth to her phone, tried to make a connection.

The screen flashed. No signal.

Portia slammed her hand on the wheel.

"We're not going to lose them on these roads. He's right on top of us." Declan glanced back again. "We'd have to get far enough ahead to pull off and hide behind an obstruction, then pray he doesn't double back and find us."

Portia gritted her teeth. "I know."

What else could they do? She prayed again, asking for more help to figure this out.

Declan pulled his gun and hit the button that rolled down the window. He twisted his torso to angle his weapon out the window and groaned. Sank back into his seat, one hand on his chest. "I don't think I can—"

Another gunshot slammed into the car. He ducked, and she bit back a scream. Declan said, "He's going to hit something vital pretty soon."

Portia's lips moved with the whisper of her prayer. She watched the road carefully, waiting for the right spot to do what she wanted. Not precisely Declan's suggestion, but it had sparked an idea that just might work.

In the wash of light from the truck's roof lamps, she saw what she needed. Dark house. Long drive.

Portia hit the gas.

Declan grabbed the roof handle.

"When I tell you, pull the emergency brake."

He put his hand on it. No arguing. No wanting an explanation. Good. There was no time for that, anyway.

Portia stayed with the angle of the road until the last second, then yanked the wheel hard to the left. She gunned it down the drive. Before they slammed into the garage door, she said "Now!"

The truck engine roared as it careened down after them. This would only work if they could get out of sight fast enough.

The second Declan pulled the emergency brake, Portia yanked the wheel hard to the right where the RV parking spot was obscured by a tree. *Please, Lord, don't let them see us.*

The back of her car swung in an arc, spraying dirt and gravel at the garage. If she could find out whose house it was later, she'd apologize. Maybe offer to have it cleaned up for them.

The truck passed them.

Portia hit the gas and drove back up the driveway, leaving the truck behind as they made their escape.

Declan turned in his seat while she gunned it back down the road they'd come up.

"Brake lights are on."

She turned her headlights on again, considering not being able to see wouldn't help her keep from sending them off a cliff. "Thank You, God."

"You prayed."

"I couldn't think of anything else to do that might actually help." She gripped the wheel while her heart pounded. "I'm far too much of a realist to consider positive thinking as effective. But prayer is so much more than that."

"Good thinking." He shifted to sit back down. "I prayed, as well. And now it doesn't look like he'll catch up too soon."

"Then we have to make sure we don't get lost in this maze of dirt streets."

"I can't believe people live out here. Doesn't it just turn into mud when it rains? And it'd be impassable in the snow."

Portia was thankful for the distraction. She needed a moment for the adrenaline to dissipate. She took a cleansing breath and said, "So they don't come up here during those times. Or they park just off the highway and get up here by four-wheeler. There are ways."

"But it's not exactly practical."

"Oh, no," she said in mock horror. "I'm stuck at home, drinking coffee and sitting by my warm fireplace. Watching the view of the mountains out the window. So sad."

"Okay, I get it."

"You've never gotten lost, just for fun?" She laughed, but it sounded nervous. They had just almost died. And they weren't completely out of the neighborhood yet.

"This is the most lost I've ever been."

"City boy."

"Maybe. I'm rethinking a lot of things these days."

Portia wasn't going to touch that. He seemed interested in her, if that look in his eye was anything to go by. But history had taught her that even if she got into a relationship, that didn't guarantee she wouldn't mess it up.

Portia gripped the wheel and said nothing. Maybe he wasn't even thinking about her in terms of a partnership. Still, even knowing fear held her in its grip, she couldn't stop herself from letting it happen. That was why she couldn't ever have that life for herself—she would only mess it up.

Declan got out his phone and had enough signal to get their GPS location on his maps app. He directed her out of the neighborhood, and they didn't see the truck again. She trusted him to lead her back to the highway while he called the local police department and made a report.

Could she trust he would guide what happened between them the same way? Even if he did, that didn't help alleviate her fears. And it didn't make something true that wasn't.

As much as she might want it to.

Maybe.

When the GPS announced the exit for Tacoma, Declan realized it was still directing them. They'd been on the freeway for miles. "I'm guessing you know your way from here." He shut it off. "You probably don't need this."

She glanced at him and smiled.

When she didn't head northwest toward Bremerton, but instead made her way northeast toward downtown Seattle, he said, "We aren't going to the office?"

She shook her head. "I'm hungry."

It was lunchtime, and she had promised him food. "I could eat."

But she hadn't exactly explained where they were going. A restaurant? Did she know she was keeping him off-kilter, not filling him in on what the plan was? Maybe it was unconscious. Not a malicious attempt to have the upper hand. He didn't think she was like that, and he tended to think the best of people. Or try to—until they proved otherwise. Why go through life always assuming the worst?

"How do you feel about slow cooker pulled pork?"

As in a slow cooker someone would set up in their own kitchen? "Where is this pork?"

"A secure residence."

"You mean a safe house." But what kind of safe house had dinner already prepared?

Portia pulled into an underground parking lot. "I'll have Lenny bring your suitcase over from the hotel before he goes home."

"I can get it. If I know where I'm bringing it to."

She shook her head and pulled into a space marked Unit 1542. "He can get it."

"Because I can't be alone?" He shot her a look so she'd know exactly how he felt about that.

"This is my house."

Declan forced back down his surprise. Her place? He watched while she worried her lip between her teeth. "What?"

"I'm wondering what to do in case there's a sniper. The windows aren't bulletproof, but it's the most secure place we have at short notice."

"So we pull the blinds. Keep the lights off if we don't absolutely need them." He knew safe house protocol, and how to protect as much as they could against rooftop snipers.

She nodded, then climbed out. They went up an elevator and she let them into the apartment. Two steps into the hall he saw framed photos. "This really is your place."

"I wasn't lying."

Apparently he hadn't all the way believed her, for some reason. She pointed to a picture on the wall. "That's my father with his unit in the first Gulf war."

Young men. Her father, the sergeant, had been older than most. Smiling faces, painted for battle. How many of them had come back changed by everything that had gone on there?

He noted the squares where pictures had been removed. Memories taken down. Things she didn't want to face every day as she left, and as she came home.

Declan smiled at her. "I was promised lunch."

She chuckled. "You can put the coffee on. The pork should be done by now. I'll make a salad."

"I'll pretend to enjoy it."

"I'll put in extra croutons."

"Excellent." He followed her through the small one-bedroom apartment into the kitchen. It gleamed. He got to work on the coffee while she set her phone on the island. She pressed a few buttons and it rang, on speaker.

"Agent Chen."

She explained what had happened and asked for Declan's things from the hotel.

"Let us know when you get there," Declan said. "I'll call the hotel manager and explain you're coming."

Lenny said, "That, plus my badge, should get me in."

"Thank you." Declan turned back to the coffeepot, which was proving quite complicated. How could there only be two buttons? When he saw the brand she drank, which was one step above construction-worker swill, he decided he'd have to pretend to enjoy that, as well.

Lenny said, "You didn't get a license plate?" Not accusing, just a question.

"Red Bronco. Nineteen ninety-seven, I think."

Declan turned to glance at Portia, but she was chopping cucumber. She could tell all that from the look they'd gotten of it? She'd already impressed him with her driving. Now she was doing it again.

"Agent Sparrow has an update for you," Lenny said. "She'll call as soon as I hang up. And I'll get you that suitcase."

"And my briefcase," Declan said. He hadn't even unpacked, so it wasn't like Lenny would have to do anything more than grab the two items. "Thanks again."

"Yep." Lenny hung up.

Portia's phone rang a second time. She tapped the screen. "Anna."

"Is he really staying at your apartment?"

Portia's face flushed a charming shade of red. She dropped the knife on the cutting board and snatched up the phone. Tapped the screen and held it to her ear. "You were on speaker." She paused. "Fine. He will be sleeping on the couch, you know that." Another pause. "I *will*." Pause. "You know that."

Portia sighed and set the phone down. "Now you can update us."

Anna's voice came through the speaker. "I do have something."

"That's good." Portia sent Declan a wry smile, her cheeks still pink.

He smiled back, and Anna said, "I went through Beth Frawley's social media accounts. She's reposted several different memories in the past year or two. Trips she's taken to a cabin. The last two with her son."

"She goes there regularly then."

Declan nodded at Portia's statement. The child was less than a year old. "Twice in eight months means she likes it."

"Or she has a reason to keep going there." Either was possible. Though, considering Beth had volunteered the information about the photograph, maybe she didn't know whether her father was using it as well.

Maybe she had no idea.

Anna said, "I checked into it. The cabin and surrounding thirty acres are all owned by a corporation that's owned by a shell company that's owned by a company with no traceable business except an account in a bank in Belize."

"Eric Frawley." The brother with no digital footprint. A sniper. Beth's uncle.

"Chris and I have been running it down since you left Beth's house, and it makes sense. Eric is off the grid. And yet here it is, family access to a cabin that can't be traced back to any of them."

Declan said, "So she lied when she said she hasn't seen her father much and hasn't seen Eric at all." He paused. "Where else would he have gone if he had a gunshot wound to his shoulder? He wouldn't have been able to go to a hospital after he raced away from the woods in that truck."

Portia nodded. "True. Beth also lied about the cabin,

which makes me disinclined to believe she hasn't seen her father," Portia said. "At the least they probably have an arrangement where she goes when no one is there, so she can be honest when she's asked about their whereabouts. Or Eric and Bill don't use it. Maybe they left it to her."

"Or she meets Bill there and knows exactly where he is right now."

He didn't like how much of a long shot this cabin was. Declan much preferred the minute-to-minute action—or waiting for action—of life at the White House. He didn't think he was cut out to be an investigator. Unpacking everything after the fact wasn't really his thing.

"We'll find out." Anna was quiet for a second, then said, "The ATF want in, so Chris and I will head over there. Take them as backup. If it's a haven for either of the Frawley brothers, then it stands to reason there could be weapons hidden on the premises."

"Keep us posted." Portia hung up and stashed the phone in her back pocket. They ate at the round dining table off the kitchen.

He took a bite of the pork and said, "This is really good. Maybe you should give me your recipe."

"I'll die before I tell. You'll never get the information out of me. It'll be passed down to my children, and to their children."

"Ah, a family secret." And not the kind that involved jail time. He smiled, finding humor where he'd never seen it before. His past wasn't something he needed to be ashamed of. She knew everything, and she hadn't judged him based on his father's actions as so many others had.

Portia sipped her coffee, watching him with those huge brown eyes. Independence. Strength. Sadness.

A red flash caught his eye. Blinked across the stoneware mug. She lowered it and the beam settled on her shirt. Right above her heart.

They'd secured the blinds.

How…

Heat sensor scope.

"Get down!"

He dived at her just as the window exploded in a spray of glass.

FOURTEEN

Portia hit the tile floor at the same time Declan did, both of them reaching for the other. Awkwardly grasping to try and save each other. He winced.

"Sorry."

Declan didn't say anything, but his face said plenty. He was in enough pain he was about to be sick.

"This way." She went first, and they slid across the floor which, thanks to Judy, her housekeeper, smelled like cleaner. There was really nowhere they'd be out of range of a sniper with heat-sensing technology. And that was the only explanation for the fact he'd shot at them through the curtains.

Shot at *her*.

Declan had seen the red dot. She'd caught a flash of it too, before they dived out of the way. If he hadn't been trained as a Secret Service agent, taught how to protect the president, she didn't think she'd be alive right now. Rifle bullets were big in a way that tore through a person and didn't leave much behind to be repaired by doctors.

That was what made sniper rifles so scary—one shot was all they needed. Often the victim didn't even see the round coming, and then it was too late.

Her phone rang. Portia slid it from the back pocket of

her pants as they moved from tile to the carpeted hallway. She wasn't getting up until she was in the bedroom. They needed walls between them and the shooter. Anything to throw off his aim.

"It's Lenny." She slid her finger across the screen. "Yeah."

"I heard the shot when I pulled up outside." His breath came in short puffs. "I'm headed up to the apartment where it came from."

"Across the street."

"Looked like it. I'll keep you posted."

"We'll be right there."

She hung up before he could object, which he would. But she wasn't about to send her teammate to apprehend a dangerous suspect with no backup.

She changed directions on the hallway floor, then got to her feet a few steps from the front door.

"Right behind you." The tightness in his voice didn't convince her he was okay.

One step into the hall, she stopped by the wall and crowded him against it. Gun ready. Face, determined. It was hard to deny someone who stood strong even in the face of scorching fire.

"You can stay here. I won't think less of you."

"That's not it," he said. "This guy is trying to kill me. And he could get away if we don't help Lenny."

Portia nodded. They took the elevator, passed the security guard in the lobby—a former marine she'd helped get the job—and yelled, "Active shooter across the street."

The guard yelled back, "Need help?"

"Get me cops and call Kitsap navy base. Ask for Director Golden, NCIS."

"On it."

Portia shoved open the front door. They would be

exposed crossing the street, but there wasn't much she could do about that. Except pray more. And so she did. Along the sidewalk, hugging the cars and SUVs parked there, using them for cover. They cut between vehicles and ducked across the street at a break in the lunchtime traffic.

The apartment building across the street had been built by the same architect a year or two before hers. The open window was on the thirteenth floor, four windows in from the far end of the building. Portia flashed her badge to the uniformed man at the desk.

"Your guy already went in." The older security guard said. "I called the cops."

She nodded, and they raced to the elevator.

On the thirteenth floor the doors slid open. Portia pressed the button to hold the doors open and listened.

She glanced back at Declan. Shook her head.

He nodded, then motioned with his fingers. She should lead, he would follow. Her left, him right.

She gave him a short nod and then stepped out.

Lenny wasn't in the hall. She couldn't see a door open at the end of the hall from this far down. Emergency exit stairs were at that end. If the shooter ran out of the apartment he could head down those, get away from them out a side door. Get lost on the street.

That meant more people in danger. And relying on the security guard to stop the man in the hall, or even the lobby, before he got away or hurt anyone.

Crack.

Portia ducked to a crouch. *Please, God, don't let Lenny be hurt.* The agent was a friend, as well as her coworker. He needed to be here to take care of his mother.

She made her way down the hall, toward a door at the end she could see now was ajar.

A man rushed out. Ball cap, bulky winter coat made for being outdoors. Facial hair she caught a flash of before he turned to the stairs, not even sparing them a glance.

"NCIS. Stop!"

He ran faster toward the stairs.

Declan passed Portia before she could race after him. He slammed into the man at the stairs, pinning him to the wall. She sprinted over and held her gun so the man could see her intent. He lifted both hands, fire in his gaze. "You're dead. Both of you."

"Then I guess it's too bad you missed. Again." Declan spun him around so he faced the wall. "Hands behind your head."

As soon as the man complied, Declan secured his hands with plastic ties and then tugged him from the wall.

She said, "Let's check on Lenny."

Portia tried not to rush, needing to stick with Declan so he wasn't overpowered by their shooter. The man might know about the bruise on Declan's chest and use it to his advantage.

Inside, the apartment was empty of furniture. The rifle was still on a short tripod, propped on a folding table pushed up to the window.

Lenny sat up on the floor, blinking. His gun was across the room.

"You good?"

"He clocked me." Lenny got to his feet with a sigh and grabbed his weapon.

The cops met them in the lobby and took over the scene, so her team could transport their suspect to the NCIS office in Lenny's car.

The man was silent the whole way, not speaking to any of them. She let Declan ride up front and sat in the back with her weapon in easy reach. She didn't want to pull it out in case he saw it as an invitation to fight her for possession of her gun.

"Not going to plead your case?" she asked.

"I know my rights. I don't have to say nothin'."

"I don't need you to say anything," she said. "I'll prove everything you've done and provide the judge with the necessary evidence to put you away for a long time."

The shooter huffed.

"Eric."

That got her a reaction. Not a big one, just a little twitch around his eye that she caught in the light of a passing car.

He'd gotten back to town in time to reach her apartment and set up across the street to take that shot. There had been enough time, but only just. Or Eric hadn't been in the truck at all, and that had been Bill. Though she figured both brothers had, given there had likely been one driver and one shooter in the vehicle.

So they'd made it back to Seattle. They'd known where Portia and Declan were. After she and Declan thought they'd lost the truck.

But how?

"Where's Bill?"

Eric said nothing. Soon enough she'd have him in an interrogation room. Armed with the right information, she would be able to bring enough leverage to get Eric to talk. It was just a question of figuring out what that leverage was going to be. A reduced sentence. The cabin remaining in their family instead of being seized by the federal government. Whatever it was, Portia was prepared to bring it to the table.

If it kept Declan safe.

Declan settled into the seat beside Portia at the interview table. He'd taken more painkillers for the giant bruise on his chest. He just didn't admit to the medic, who had come over from the other side of the base to look at Lenny's head, that it hurt this badly still.

Eric Frawley yawned. The jaw-cracking, lip-smacking kind.

"Lovely." Declan shook his head. "Tell us where Bill is, and you can go to holding. Get some sleep." Wherever they held prisoners on base. Was it the brig? He should ask Portia later.

Eric sighed, his big belly expanding as he breathed. "Haven't seen him."

Portia said, "Not since he was driving, and you were shooting at us out the window of a red Bronco, that is. But, no. Other than that you haven't seen him."

"I see you." He leaned across the table, all of his attention on Declan. "And Bill says you're gonna die for what your daddy did."

Declan said quietly, "What my father did has nothing to do with me."

"I take my vengeance on the children's children's children. It's in the Bible."

"Pretty sure that's *not* what it says." At least, not the way Eric was applying it. Declan was pretty sure only God—under a now obsolete Old Testament system—had said that particular phrase. And he was also pretty sure it was about the consequences of sin, not judgment. Jesus had washed all that away with His sacrifice.

Portia said, "We're not going to let you do that. We have you, and we're going to find Bill."

"Your friend here is still gonna die. You all are. The United American Citizens will overthrow this system of government, and all you little sheep will die." The whites around his eyes were almost yellow. The row of teeth he flashed were the same color. "Won't be long now."

The antigovernment group was up to something.

He needed to contact Secret Service intelligence. Even if they knew about the group already, they needed to be informed that a possible plan was in the works. A domestic organization threatening American citizens? No one wanted that.

"Tell us what they have planned," Portia said. "I'll see if I can get you a deal. A reduced sentence. But only if you help us."

Eric snorted. "So you can stop a plan I helped design?" His thick chest shifted with the force of his chuckle.

Declan said, "It won't seem so funny when you're serving consecutive life sentences."

"Because you think we'll fail."

"I have no doubt you'll be stopped. Do you know how many attacks are foiled in American cities every year? Law enforcement across the country work hard to keep us safe, and you're crazy if you think you can outsmart them."

"Never said I wasn't crazy. Or at least paranoid. That's what makes me so good at plans." He tapped a finger against his temple. "I think of all the angles."

Portia said, "The first Gulf war, right?"

Declan sat quietly and let the man answer her question in his own time.

He blinked and focused on her. Shrugged.

"My dad served back then." She gave a battalion number.

Eric whistled. "Those guys were hard-core."

She nodded. "I knew a lot of them. And a lot who didn't come home. If they did they were changed. The government didn't do them any favors, taking so long to wake up to PTSD. Seems like the bureaucracy doesn't like to admit when they're at fault."

"It's all on them, what happened to our boys."

"My father felt much the same as you do." Portia paused. "Right up until the day he killed himself."

Eric said, "Your old man did that?"

Portia nodded.

She'd told Declan her father had been sick, and that was what had killed him. Was she lying to this guy, just trying to get on his good side so he would open up to her? He didn't think she was the kind of person who would use manipulation tactics that were so blatant. But in the interview room, what rules were there? Could she promise whatever she wanted, and tell whatever lie she needed to, all to get the suspect to talk?

Another thing Declan didn't like about investigation work. Not because he thought he was morally superior. But it took a certain kind of person to draw the right information out of an interviewee. People lied. They twisted their words. Told others what they wanted to—about themselves and people they came across—and it would take skill to discern what was fabrication and what was the truth.

Portia was impressing him yet again. She was fantastic at this job, and it was hard to believe what Anna had told him was true—that her ATF ex-boyfriend had expected her to give it up. When it was so clearly her calling? Sure, she might want to have children someday, but the idea of expecting her to just quit her job without taking her wishes—and all the other options—into account just wasn't right. And it wasn't the way to inure her to doing anything.

Eric leaned back in his seat, eyeing Portia like she might be his kind of people. Probably exactly what she wanted. "The United American Citizens will finish its work on this earth. Even if that means we go out in a blaze of fire and glory. It's the right thing to do to a government that cares not one whit for its citizens."

Declan wasn't going to debate the merits—or lack thereof—of the government with this guy. Not when it wasn't likely he could change the man's mind. Determined didn't quite cover his fanaticism.

He decided to take a risk by dangling a carrot as it were, and said, "If you give us Bill, we'll leave your little weapons sales group alone. As a favor." He didn't know if he could use his pull to make this happen, but it was worth trying. The UAC was going down. Eric and his friends selling weapons were small fish. And after they lost all their contacts, he would make sure their business failed.

Declan saw Portia glance at him, but he didn't meet her gaze.

Eric said, "Give up my own brother?"

"He could compromise what UAC has planned. You already drew attention to yourself, trying to kill me. Bill could mess things up even more."

Eric's beard shifted as he worked his mouth back and forth. "Wish I knew where he was."

They already had Chris and Anna checking out the cabin. But if Bill wasn't holed up there, if he was waiting to take Eric back with him, they needed to know where he was.

Declan glanced at the clock. It had been a couple of hours since Anna spoke with them. Had they checked it out already? If it was empty—or if Anna and Chris had already detained Bill—they needed to know.

"We should take a break." Declan pushed his chair back and stood. "I need coffee, and he isn't giving us anything." He tried to sound petulant so Portia could use his attitude as a springboard to connect more with the man. Anything that might help.

He walked out, heading toward the desks so he could contact the other agents. Find out if they'd discovered anything. Portia's phone was ringing when he got there, so Declan snapped it up. "Agent Finch's phone."

He heard her behind him. "What are you—"

Declan held up one finger, listening to what the ATF agent was saying. Then he moved the phone away from his mouth and relayed the information. "The ATF got to the rendezvous point, where they were supposed to meet Chris and Anna. Their car is there, but not them. The doors are open, and there's blood on the seats."

FIFTEEN

Portia pushed aside the frustration that Declan had answered her desk phone. Being annoyed with him might be valid, but it wasn't going to help. Chris and Anna were *both* missing? Blood on the seats?

She turned away and pulled in a breath. Call Lenny—no, she had Declan here. Lenny had been injured earlier. She glanced at her phone and saw it was seven in the evening. He'd be done at the ER by now. She didn't need to pull her injured teammate in when regular work hours were over, and he was taking care of his sick mother. Lenny was home, and at least someone on the team should be rested for tomorrow morning.

Not to mention they also had a possible threat on their hands. Chris's and Anna's disappearance—and possible kidnapping—needed to be her team's priority. Her and Declan's priority.

ATF could take care of the threat.

"Give me the phone."

His eyes widened, but she wasn't going to apologize for her tone. He passed over the handset. "Get me Agent Mason."

There was a two-second pause, and the agent said, "Yes, ma'am."

It was no longer simply Declan, or her, in danger.

Now it was members of her team also. Which meant she needed to wake up Lenny just to check he was all right.

Steve's voice came over the line. "Portia?"

"Agent Stringer and I are headed over to this rendezvous point, and we'll bring a forensics team." Squire was probably still in his lab working. "I want one of your agents there to give me an update when I arrive. After we process the scene, we'll head up to the cabin."

"Don't know where it is. Someone will need to get the information off Agent Sparrow's computer, because they were going to fill us in when we got there."

Portia sighed. Another job for Squire—one that would slow down their progress. Squire would have to work here before he drove to the scene to process the car.

She pulled out her cell phone and emailed him while she was on the phone with Steve. "Okay, on it." She paused to gather her thoughts. "Eric Frawley hasn't said much, but he mentioned the United American Citizens. He indicated they have an operation coming up. If Declan and I go after Chris and Anna, can you guys take point on running that down?"

The last thing they needed was for an attack to happen while they were looking for their teammates. Was that why Bill had taken them? This could all be an engineered distraction. But that was precisely why she needed ATF on it. The stolen weapons and this threat could both be part of their case. Hers was about her people—Declan included.

Steve said, "That group has been on our radar for a while. The news Eric is in the know about anything they're up to is new to me, though. Thanks for passing that on."

"No problem."

Squire rounded the end of the desks, gave her a chin lift and sat at Anna's desk. He'd run his hands through his hair so that it stuck up in handfuls all over his head.

She said to Steve, "You're aware of a possible threat."

"When is there not a possible threat in the works from some group, or an individual with a grudge? But UAC has been in our sights. If they're connected to these stolen weapons by way of the Frawley brothers...well then, this attack could be what they need the guns for."

Portia was glad that wasn't her job. And that there were professional men and women in this country who were dedicated to keeping its citizens safe. She glanced at Declan. He was top of that echelon. First tier. Up there protecting the president 24/7. It was an admirable pursuit.

Hers was a little more down-to-earth. Like a police detective, just that she worked on cases that were all navy-related.

Portia said, "I think Bill might've taken Chris and Anna, or had them abducted—maybe even by United American Citizens—to distract us from whatever they're gearing up for."

"Sounds right to me. Bill doesn't seem to be the point man. He's not a central figure. He just gets attention because he posts on blogs, so his name is out there."

"Maybe a scapegoat."

"That's what I'd do with him if I was in charge of it," Steve said. "I'll make a call. Have Eric transferred to our custody. He'll tell me what he knows about UAC and their plans."

Portia wanted to question that, considering she hadn't gotten very far with the man. Even bonding over the first Gulf war. Still, she wasn't going to get between a man and his professional ego. "You might want to look at Sebastian Mallory, as well. There could be a connection."

"Okay," Steve said. "It's in both our interests to find Bill."

"Agreed."

"Anything else you need from me?"

She said, "Not unless you can get scent dogs to that trailhead faster than I can."

"Not likely."

"Then keep me posted."

"Will do. And I'll leave a man here to babysit the scene."

"Thanks." She hung up, glad to know that all the evidence was going to be preserved until they made it to the parking lot.

"I don't mind driving," Declan said. "You look wiped."

"I am." But he was the one who'd been shot yesterday.

Today had been another crazy day, and now it was turning out to be a crazy evening. She made the call for scent dogs. The marines had the best canine unit, and that wasn't just navy pride talking. They were top-notch, and she loved watching them work. Too bad it was because two of her team members were missing.

God, keep them safe. He had kept her head above water so far through this. She had no doubt He had the power to hold her up even if this turned out to be the worst type of situation. Maybe they were already dead. But she didn't want to think like that.

"Let's go."

Declan nodded.

"Squire?"

"Anna changed her password, but I got in." He grinned. "She uses random nouns but when she changes it she uses the next two letters in the alphabet, so umbrella and sandwich becomes something starting with a *V* and something with a *T* so—"

"Squire."

He closed his mouth. Then said, "I emailed you the

cabin's address. Plus a GPS location. There isn't exactly a road to get up there."

That sounded like the perfect vacation home to her. Portia's father had owned that rickety fishing boat, but a cabin would be cozy. And a fireplace? Hot coffee and a warm comforter on the couch while she read a book.

Declan cleared his throat.

Portia snapped out of that very sleepy daydream. "Let's go." She spun on her heel and they headed out.

"I'll be right behind you."

She waved back to Squire over her shoulder and hit the button for the elevator.

"I might be asking you sometime about that daydream you just had. It seemed nice."

They climbed on the elevator together.

He said, "Am I invited?"

"To my daydream?"

He shot her a look, like she should know what he meant.

"I'll tell you all about it," Portia said. "As soon as we find Chris and Anna."

"Drew the short straw, huh?" Portia strode over to the ATF agent on duty at the crime scene. The guy shut the door of his vehicle and met them halfway.

Declan frowned past her at the car Chris and Anna had been driving. Door open, dome light still on. Was this just how the ATF had found it? On the drive over to the trailhead parking lot, Portia had run the gamut of emotions from anger to just plain scared. Now he saw she was falling back on that cop humor that kept them detached from the reality of the awful things they saw.

The ATF agent said, "I'm Callan. You're Portia Finch?"

She flashed her badge. Declan did the same.

"Car was like this when we found it." He crossed the short distance to the vehicle.

Declan's lips twitched as he followed. Maybe he was falling back on cop humor as well, otherwise it wouldn't be funny that the guy had just said exactly what he was thinking. That, or he was past tired. It was late.

Portia used the light from her phone to get a better look at the car. "Front seat's covered in blood."

Declan opened the passenger door. "Over here looks clear."

"I'm thinking head wound, maybe. They bleed a lot, and there's no sign of a knife or gun. Material on the seat is intact."

She was careful not to touch anything, or let her hair get in the car. Portia didn't want to contaminate the crime scene, and neither did he. But last time when they'd opened a glove box, the discovery of a gun had led to a breakthrough in the case.

Declan used the corner of his phone as a lever to pop the latch. The glove box popped open. No gun. "Shame." That would've been good. Though what help it might've been, he didn't know. One weapon wasn't likely to help when they needed clues as to where Bill might've taken Chris and Anna. If indeed it was Bill who had taken them.

Portia said, "If Chris has to help Anna, he can't take on Bill as easily. And vice versa. It's in Bill's best interest for them to just go along with what he says."

"So he hurt one, and took them both. For what reason?" Declan knew about her distraction theory, but kidnapping two NCIS agents?

"Maybe he only planned to take one. Or they fought back."

"If he really is staying at the cabin, it'd be a serious coincidence they were at the trailhead together. He could've been leaving or arriving in a vehicle. If he loaded them into it, he could've taken them anywhere by now." It'd been hours since they were taken.

Whoever was bleeding could be dead already. Or they might not have much time.

Declan backed up and shone the light on his phone at the ground. "Callan," he called out. "How many of your people walked around the car?"

"That side, not many. We just looked in the driver's side, where all the blood is."

Declan studied the mass of footprints from the car, headed toward the sign where the trail started. The cabin was two miles up the side of this mountain, and then another quarter mile into the trees.

That was far to walk if a person was injured.

Declan couldn't know for sure if they'd gone up the trail. There were a couple of cars here, apart from their three. Even though the bulk of footprints led that way, it was a guess more than anything else. This place could get a ton of foot traffic for all he knew.

A truck pulled up, a dog crate in the back. The man driving was in military camo and mud-covered boots. He jumped out, a leash in one hand.

Portia shook his hand. "Good to see you." She introduced him and Declan, and the guy moved away to put down the tailgate. He hopped in the bed of the truck and opened the crate. The dog's tongue was all Declan could see in the dark.

The man climbed out and took two steps back. "*Hier.*"

At the German command to come, the dog trotted from the crate, jumped off the truck bed and sat beside his master's left leg. The man gave him a head scratch. More tongue.

"Declan, this is Justin." She motioned to the man, then the dog. "And Stella."

Declan shook the marine's hand. "Stringer."

"Let's head to the cabin," Portia said. "I want to know if they're there."

The forensics van pulled into the lot. Squire waved to them, and parked.

The marine and his dog spent some time by the bloody car, and Portia pulled a sealed bag out of hers, along with a small case—a first-aid kit. She held up the sealed bag. "This is from Anna's gym bag."

The marine let the dog sniff the material in the bag, then the ground. After giving the command it took only seconds before he was at the trailhead and moving fast.

Declan checked the GPS on his phone, tracking the dog's route all the way to the location he'd marked for the cabin.

The dog stayed on the trail the whole way there.

"They're at the cabin, aren't they?"

Portia nodded. Both of them were in a loose jog, keeping pace about a quarter mile back from the dog and the marine, the flashlight the man held bobbing with each step. "The question is, what kind of state are they going to be in when we get there?"

"And how much of a fight is Bill going to put up?"

"The last thing we need is a hostage situation."

Would the marine and the dog be able to help? The marine he figured was likely armed and would lend a hand. The dog might not have been trained in suspect takedown. Not if she was a scent dog. It was hard to know, which meant prior to approaching the cabin they had to stop and figure out how to approach this.

Justin called out in a low voice, "Your agent definitely walked this path."

It wasn't absolute confirmation that Anna was inside

the cabin. Declan couldn't see any lights, but it looked like the door was open. He figured without actually walking through the door and checking inside, the dog couldn't say if she was there. Just that she'd headed in this direction.

"Stella will stay here. I'll provide backup," the marine said, motioning to his dog.

"Thank you." Declan was glad it wasn't just him and Portia going up against a suspect who could be holed up in a cabin he'd outfitted with who knew what defenses.

"I'll take point." She glanced at the marine. "You're with me. Declan, take the back door." Without waiting for either of them to confirm, Portia strode out into the clearing in front of the cabin. "Bill Frawley, this is NCIS. Come out with your hands up!" Her voice rang out across the clearing.

"Portia?" A voice called back.

"Chris?" She started to run. Declan followed, tossing out the plan where he went around the back.

He yelled, "Is Bill in there?"

"No! He's gone."

They ran inside, and the marine shone his flashlight. The dog wandered the room, sniffing.

Chris was propped against one wall. Furniture was sparse, and it looked like there'd been a struggle.

Blood coated the young man's leg.

Declan flipped the lid on the first-aid kit, crouching on the left side where his wound was. He ripped open a gauze pad and pressed it against the wound. Chris hissed. Declan said "Sorry."

"Bill?" Portia asked. "And Anna?"

Chris's gaze darkened. The sheen of tears in his eyes. "He left me here and took her."

"Where did he go?"

"I don't know. But he said the only way we're going to get her back is if we trade her for Declan."

SIXTEEN

Portia knocked on the hospital room door. When Chris called, “Come in,” she opened it and stepped inside.

“All stitched up?”

He looked a little pale, but better than he had at the cabin. “Yep. Squire said he’ll stay with me while I heal. Sleep on my couch. I’m kinda scared, actually. Although my TV has been having issues connecting to the internet, so I figure he’ll fix that. And probably my dishwasher too.”

Portia grinned and handed over a bottle of his favorite soda.

“Sweet.”

She settled on the bed beside his right leg.

“I’m guessing you want me to walk you through what happened.” When she nodded, he said, “I’ve been running through it in my head, over and over. I just can’t figure out where he’s going to take her on foot in the middle of nowhere.” He paused. “Unless he stashed his truck somewhere we didn’t see it?”

That big red truck should’ve stuck out from any hiding spot, and yet none of them had seen it.

“How did it all go down?”

Chris ran a hand through his mussed hair, his young

face twisting. The rookie was twenty-four, which felt like a lifetime ago to her. Had she ever laughed as much as he did?

He said, "We'd been parked for a while."

"Who drove?"

"I did."

So all the blood in the front seat had been his? It was good to know Anna wasn't hurt—as far as she knew. But thinking about Chris dripping blood all the way up that trail wasn't a happy thought.

"What time did you get there?"

"Just before midnight. The ATF were half an hour behind us." Chris shook his head. "He must've known we would be there. That we would show up."

"He could've known Declan and I talked to Beth. That we'd find out about the cabin from her. That's enough for him to lie in wait for one of us to show up." Especially considering his brother had followed them back to Seattle to take another shot. "And if it wasn't Declan then he'd simply take whoever it was and do this trade deal for him that you mentioned."

"I just can't help thinking that if I'd paid more attention, and not been so deep in our conversation, then I'd never have let him get the door open that fast and get the jump on me."

Portia kind of agreed with him. Though she couldn't say unequivocally that the same thing wouldn't have happened to her. Still, he didn't need that right now. Not when, if the worst happened, he'd have to live with the guilt of it. He had enough with just this.

She said, "It was dark. You didn't think to be aware of a possible ambush."

"I should've thought of it."

"There was no reason to, Chris. It doesn't make you a bad agent."

Agents who'd been doing this job longer than him had quit over something like this. It was hard for people to trust their own abilities and instincts after a teammate was harmed. More so if the person believed different actions could've changed the outcome.

He looked away. Maybe not convinced, but she figured he needed to think on it. Hopefully he had his head on straight enough that he'd come out solid in the end. The alternative would be a waste of a rookie agent who had a serious amount of promise in him. Chris could have a long and impressive career. If he could pass over this snag without it tripping him up.

Lord, help Anna. She'd been praying nonstop for hours. And she would keep doing it until her teammate was returned. Not traded for Declan. Portia wasn't looking for anything other than both of them safe, and Bill in custody like Eric and Mallory were.

Keep her safe. Help me find her. Show me how to get to her.

Bill might be gearing up to contact Declan, to offer the trade. He was aware of that and waiting. Alert, like the rest of them. But Declan's job was different. She knew he had it in him to give himself up to Bill in exchange for Anna. Too bad for him there was no way she was going to let that occur. She didn't give in to demands.

"Sometimes things happen, and there's nothing we can do about it," she told him. "It's what you do with it that counts. Do you let the blow knock you down, or do you come back swinging twice as hard?"

His thoughtful eyes studied the knit blanket the hospital staff had laid on him.

Portia figured one of these days she was going to have

to take her own advice. After her father's death, she'd been knocked down. She'd let that whole situation lay her flat, and had she really gotten up? Emotionally, probably not. She was still grieving.

Declan, and what was happening between them, was the closest she'd come so far to getting up. To trusting someone again. It hadn't exactly been betrayal, what her father had done. Yes, he'd been sick. He'd died. She didn't like how he'd…

Portia swallowed the lump in her throat, hardly even able to think what he'd done.

It had felt like betrayal. And she'd shut herself off from everyone.

Steve had seen it. Her team hadn't called her on it. The director had asked if she needed to talk to a professional. Was it possible all she'd needed was Declan? She didn't even know what it was about him that made her feel this way.

She got up from the bed, and Chris said, "Will you keep me updated on what's happening?"

"Of course." She strode to the door, and the hallway. The waiting room where Declan had settled into a chair. Head back against the wall, eyes closed. Not an uncommon sight in a hospital. How he could sleep with all the noise was anyone's guess.

She crossed the room to him. Before she got close enough to tap his shoulder and let him know it was time to go, his eyes opened. He shot up out of the chair. "What is it? What happened?"

Of course he thought something was wrong. All she could do was think how long it had been since things in her life had been right.

"Portia?"

She walked right into the hug and wrapped her arms

around his middle, trying to be careful of his bruise. A second later he circled her in his strong grip. The breadth of his shoulders was like a safe haven. A sanctuary from everything that was wrong.

"We'll find her."

She nodded against his chest.

"Hey."

She lifted her gaze and he laid his cheek on hers. Pressed his lips there. The sigh came from deep in her soul. Portia burrowed closer to him, still keeping her arms loose, and took a minute to regroup before she said "We should go."

"Back to the office?"

She nodded. "I'm expecting an update from the ATF, and I need to see what Squire found in the car. And the cabin."

"He's been busy."

"It's our best shot at a lead." She moved to pull away, but his arms didn't loosen. She looked up at him.

Declan said, "I'm sorry for the reason, but I'm glad for what just happened."

That might not have made sense, but she understood. "Me too." She'd sought him out for comfort, and he seemed to understand how rare that was.

Declan leaned back in the conference-room chair and sipped some of the strongest coffee he'd ever tasted. Portia wasn't messing around, and she certainly hadn't been when she'd made it.

She frowned at Steve, who also sat at the table. "That's completely inadmissible."

"How I got this intel doesn't matter. You want to find your agent, right? Putting Mallory and Eric on the same prisoner transport and placing a recording device between them was my decision."

"No court is going to admit that to evidence."

Steve sighed. "So we make a case that's strong enough we don't need it to convict Mallory, Eric or Bill."

She didn't look convinced.

"Do you want to hear the recording or not?"

Portia shrugged. "Do they say where Bill took Anna?"

"No," Steve said through gritted teeth.

Declan set a hand on Portia's arm, and said to Steve, "Please play the tape."

The ATF agent jerked his head down in a short nod. He pressed Play on his phone, instead of pulling out a recorder. Declan's brain had to catch up.

He looked at the clock on the wall. Almost six in the morning. Had he slept at all last night other than snatches of time, here and there? Portia had done the same, switching off who drove and who slept. Who ordered food, and who crashed on the break room couch. She looked about as wiped as he felt.

The speaker on Steve's phone crackled, and then a male voice said, "…better do it."

Pause. Then a reply. "There's no one else." Eric's voice was tight. "Bill's the only one not dead or in custody to make the deal."

Declan sat up in the chair.

"UAC is going to kill all of us." That was Mallory.

"Not much we can do about that. Their guys in lockup will make sure we don't talk."

"So you're just going to roll over and let them?" Mallory continued, "I can't believe you guys messed up so badly. All because you wanted to get Declan Stringer on your turf. Turns out it's harder to kill him than you thought, huh?"

Eric was quiet for a moment, then said, "We would have gotten him."

Mallory snorted. "You should have hit him with your rifle the first time you had him in your sights. Then you go and chase him in the truck. And how were you going to draw out his brother, anyway?"

"Same way we got him here. Identifying his brother's body."

"Pay the sheriff off again? That it?"

Cold moved through Declan, despite the hot coffee. Portia shot him a commiserating look. She understood what his brother meant to him, despite the strain in their relationship. Now hearing the sheriff had been bought off?

When Nicholas got back stateside, Declan was going to seek him out. See if they could repair things between them. Start fresh.

He needed to move past this stress. The sick feeling wasn't leaving his gut anytime soon. Being targeted for what his father had done. Knowing now these men had gone to such lengths for this personal vendetta. Like he could have changed his father's actions?

Mallory said, "You guys are idiots."

"His father ruined our family." Eric's voice boomed through the speakers.

A third person said, "Pipe down, both of you."

Eric said, "You're the one who promised UAC all those weapons."

"We were good for them."

"It was insane. No wonder it went sideways."

"Hasn't yet," Mallory said. "And it won't if your brother makes the morning ferry."

Steve clicked a button on his phone. "Things degenerate from there, until one of the officers transporting them wades in again and they shut down."

"Bill's the only one who can make the deal," Declan stated, paraphrasing what had been said. He needed to process it aloud to try and figure out the implications. Mallory had been a source of information. But now it was clear he was in on it.

Declan tapped his finger on the table. "He'd have to stash Anna somewhere in order to get to this ferry meet."

Would he contact Declan after he'd done this bit of business? He might kill Anna and still attempt to make the exchange just to draw Declan out. He didn't think Mallory had been in charge, but they were clearly working together. "Frank Parsons must have been part of their group, as well. Maybe a new addition, one Bill and Eric decided was expendable in order to get me here."

Portia said, "If we can scope out the terminals, we might see him board a ferry this morning. If we can follow, we should be able to effect a takedown."

"I want whoever he's dealing with," Steve said. "ATF will be running this operation. We wait until the deal is done, and then we sweep up all the players. That's the only way we'll know who we're dealing with."

"And while you're all waiting," Portia said, "my agent spends more time scared for her life, wondering when we're going to find her. *If* we're going to find her."

"You can have Bill."

"After you're done?" She shot him a look that said that wasn't much of a help.

Steve shook his head. "First."

Portia's eyes widened. Declan figured that was the only concession Steve was going to make. He didn't seem unaffected by the fact Anna had been kidnapped, but he was still going to do what was in the best interests of the ATF. Not in a territorial way. Steve was just doing his job.

Portia shifted in her chair. "This better work."

It was a long shot, but they all knew how important it was to her to find Anna. For every member of her team.

Steve stood, pushing his chair back from the table. "I'll go get everything set up and let you know where to be."

He left the room, and Declan and Portia both stood. She glanced at him. "You okay?"

He could've asked her the same thing. "I'll feel better when Anna has been found."

Half an hour later they were stood inside the Bremerton ferry terminal. Most of the crowd were dressed in suits as they were, making them blend in with morning commuters headed into Seattle to work. It was still early yet, making large coffees a necessity. And not out of place.

Declan waited, listening to the ATF chatter in his earpiece. He and Portia had opted to stay together. They could be here for hours, watching to see if Bill came through. ATF agents were getting on every ferry that left. They were also stationed at the Seattle terminal where agents were riding every ferry that came this direction.

He was impressed Steve had been able to pull it together in such a short time.

Portia sipped her coffee, stood beside him in a loose stance. Ready to move at a second's notice.

"Anything?"

She didn't shake her head. "No sign of Bill. He could've shaved his beard since Chris saw him. We'll have to be careful."

Declan nodded.

Portia took a step forward.

"What—?"

She waved him off. “No way.”

He moved after her, aware his stance was protective. It was ingrained in him. Too late to change that now. She would have a world-class protective detail at her back, and Declan would make sure he got plenty more of those hugs in the future. Never mind that technically he was the one in danger.

“Portia.”

In his ear, Steve barked, “What is it?”

“I don’t believe it.” Portia didn’t slow. Didn’t look back at him. She continued to weave through the crowd with more and more purpose to her stride. “It’s Beth Frawley. She’s here.”

SEVENTEEN

Portia and Declan waved their badges at the attendant and stepped onto the walkway that would take them to the ferry. Underneath, cars drove onto the ship for the journey to Seattle. Overhead low gray clouds drizzled rain, the kind that soaked into everything she was wearing and made her hair frizz into tiny curls when it dried.

Beth headed immediately inside on the ferry, out of the rain. No one remained on deck. Portia prayed Beth wouldn't immediately look out the window and spot them. She headed down the side of the ship, between the wall of windows and the railing. Usually it would be occupied by at least some people—tourists or families—watching the view. Not today.

Beyond where Beth went inside, they did the same. Then Portia doubled back, so they'd be able to observe her from the far side of the room.

Chatter on the radios caught up to what was happening. The ATF regrouped, adjusting for the fact Bill's daughter was here. And it seemed like Bill himself was not.

Which meant Beth was now their best shot at finding Anna.

Declan tapped her arm and they slipped into two unforgiving plastic seats. How did people sit on these for an hour? He pulled out his phone and swiped through screens, not looking at anything in particular. These days it was unusual for someone not to be on their phone, so she was glad he had chosen that to try and blend in. Pretend they were relaxed, as opposed to watching everything that was going on.

Which was precisely what Portia was doing.

Beth sat by a window across the room, also not on her phone. She wiped her palms on the legs of her skinny pants, clutching her large purse to her side with her elbow. What was inside that she was guarding? Money? A weapon? If she was here to make the deal on Bill's behalf, she clearly wasn't used to doing so.

Portia figured it was more likely that she had money. That the group comprised of Mallory, Bill and Eric—and evidently Beth in a pinch—were attempting to purchase weapons from someone. Were the weapons on board the ferry? They could be in the trunk of a car. Beth could purchase the keys from whoever showed up to meet her, and simply drive the vehicle off the ferry at the other end.

It was a slick way to do business—provided they didn't draw attention to themselves. Too bad for Beth this was a sting operation. She wasn't going to walk out of here free, and neither was whoever showed up to—

A man walked toward her bench seat. Portia watched him lumber along. Bulky jacket and jeans. Work boots. Portia didn't recognize him.

The man passed Beth and continued on.

"Anything?" Declan said the word under his breath but didn't look up. Still, by all appearances, engrossed in his phone. The way so many people were these days. Young and old, completely oblivious of the world around them. Far too worried about the virtual world that they wound up taking too many risks. Most put their lives in danger routinely, never aware of the potential threat around them. Safety had gone out the window.

"Nope."

Beth shifted in her seat, then looked at her phone. Checking the time? They had about forty-five minutes until the ferry reached the Seattle terminal. Maybe the meet wouldn't even take place on the ship. Perhaps Beth was commuting to somewhere else.

Portia could pick out the ATF agents stationed inside the ferry seating area. Maybe it was just that she was also a fed—albeit a military one. She didn't think they stuck out to anyone who didn't know what to look for. On the outside, all those suits and ties just made them look like commuters. They'd all have dressed differently if it was the middle of the afternoon rather than eight in the morning.

"Movement at two o'clock."

Portia flicked her gaze to the side but didn't turn her head. A burly man with a full stomach sat across from Beth. Shaved cheeks, no stubble. Denim shirt, and cargo pants. Military-style boots.

"Marine," Portia said. "I'd guess a staff sergeant."

Declan said, "You can tell that just by looking?"

Portia scrunched her lips up to her nose as a yes. An ATF agent came over the radio. "We're running his photo against the navy's database."

"Copy that," Portia answered. "Anyone close enough to hear what they're saying?"

Beth and the man had started a conversation. The short back and forth of small talk. An occasional nod.

The man motioned to her purse and said something.

"Did you bring the money?" one of the ATF agents said, reading the marine's lips from his position.

Beth nodded. Asked a question.

"I didn't catch that," the agent said.

But Beth pulled a manila envelope from her purse and held it out with shaky fingers. The man slid it into a pocket on the leg of his pants. He dipped into another pocket and pulled out a small silver key on a single key ring.

Beth took the key, her hand moving toward her purse. At the last second she didn't, but slipped the key into her pocket instead. *Good for her.* A purse could be stolen much easier than something could be lifted from a pocket. Whatever the key was for, it had value. Which meant it was worth safeguarding.

The marine got up and moved away.

The call came over the radio. "All positions, move in."

Portia stood and started walking. She and Declan were with the couple of agents tasked to grab Beth. The rest would split off and detain the marine. This needed to be done as quickly and quietly as possible, and without endangering any of the innocent bystanders. The last thing they needed were injuries—to anyone.

Beth hadn't gotten up from her seat. There were still at least fifteen minutes until they pulled in to Seattle. Maybe she was planning on staying put until then. Dispersing with the crowd of commuters.

"Beth?" Portia had her hand close to her gun, but not close enough it was obvious she could pull it out at any second. She was trusting the fact Beth wasn't going to get violent.

"Oh!" The woman blanched, then covered it. "It's… Agent Finch, right?"

Portia's smile didn't last long. "You'll need to come with me. We need to speak with you about the transaction you just made." No pretense. No beating around the bush.

Beth said, "I don't know what you're talking about."

"Don't play games with me, Beth. Your father sent you here to make a deal with that man. He has one of my people hostage, and she could be hurt. He might even have killed her. Now you tell me everything, including where your father is *right now.* Or I'm going to push for the ATF to file charges of illegal weapons trafficking." She paused. "You'll never see your son again."

Beth's eyes filled with tears that spilled over onto her cheeks. "He… I…"

Portia steeled herself against any empathy inside her. "Tell me where Anna is. That's the only way you'll even have a chance to go home to your son."

Declan watched as Beth's face twisted with anger. "You can't do that! You can't keep me from my son!"

Portia stood her ground. "You'd be surprised what leverage I have when a federal agent has been kidnapped. Right now you're the only one who might know where she is."

"Like I know anything about that." Her voice was high. Shrill.

Declan winced. She'd seemed nice enough at her house. Now Beth was a snarling mess of running tears and anger. Like a feral cat that had been cornered. He said, "Where is your father now?"

She glanced aside. "Like I should know?"

"You're lying." Portia hesitated. She probably wanted to arrest Beth but processing her and getting her in an interview room would take time. Time Anna might not have. It had been hours since she was taken. They had no idea if she was all right, or if she might be hurt.

Declan pressed his lips together and prayed while Portia pressured Beth for her father's whereabouts. He prayed they would find Anna. That the worst—or anything else nearly equally as bad that would leave the young woman scarred for the rest of her life—hadn't happened. That it wouldn't happen before they could get to her.

"He just called me. He didn't say where he was, just to come here and meet that guy. My dad said he was a friend of his, and that I should give him the envelope. He was going to give me something back."

"You didn't realize this was an illegal deal?" Declan asked. "You know your father. And yet none of this raised any red flags for you?" She didn't seem that dense and still, here they were. Why would a young woman like this jeopardize her future, and her son's, for what she thought was a favor for her dad?

Beth's feral stare landed on him. "I know who you are, *Declan Harris*." She said his name like it was a curse word. "The Declan whose father ruined our family. He took everything we had, and we never got any of it back."

She was younger than him, not born yet when it all happened. She must have been told about it by Bill, or Eric, or both.

He said, "You think I'm responsible for what my father did? I was a kid."

"Don't matter," she spat back. "Two families feuding. It's like, historical and stuff."

"We're not feuding. Your father and uncle are trying to kill me."

Beth's mouth curled into a sneer.

"This isn't helping your case," Portia said. "Unless you want to be in prison until your son is an adult, you need to tell me where your father is. Right now."

She shrugged. "Don't know. Samuel's dad has him, so what do I care?" Her façade slipped a little. "Put me in prison if you want. You'll never find him. So make your threats. See if I care."

She might not care if she went to prison, but she cared that she would be away from her son. Despite her attempt at bravado, that was the way to get to her.

"United American Citizens." Portia stared at the young woman, putting the pieces together. "He's with them, isn't he? You're the connection to them."

Beth blinked, but tried to pass off her surprise. "So what?"

"That means you're in this deeper than we thought. And your son is going to grow up as part of that group. Nothing but a pawn in their scheme. I can hand you over to the ATF right now, and they'll get the information they need from you."

"Don't know nothin'."

Declan said, "Because you want plausible deniability, or they don't trust you with the information?"

"He trusted me with having his baby," Beth snapped back at them. "So what about the rest of it? Like I care about plans and invasions."

Invasions? *Please tell me she's joking.* Portia glanced at him, sharing the sentiment. It was written all over her face.

Portia held out her hand. "Your phone."

"I'm not giving you—"

Portia touched the radio in her ear. Unnecessary, considering that it wasn't part of how it functioned. But from Beth's face, she realized what it meant when Portia said, "This is Agent Finch. I need someone from ATF to take this suspect into custody. She has ties with United American Citizens."

Beth blanched. "I don't know anything! I'm not telling them squat!"

Declan wasn't sure which was true and which was her blustering. Either she was aware of something or she wasn't. Maybe Beth didn't know what she knew. Whatever the case, the ATF would get to the bottom of it. And hopefully whatever that group had planned, the feds would stop it.

While Declan and Portia found Anna.

"The *phone*," Portia repeated. "Or you'll be taking the risk your son gets picked up by child services when the feds raid UAC's compound and his father is arrested."

Beth swiped away more tears and handed over a brand-new smartphone.

"The code?"

She swiped a pattern on the home screen. "What are you gonna look at?"

"Your call history," Portia said, already swiping through the screens right to where she needed to go. The phone was tilted so Beth could see what she was doing.

"We need your dad's number," Declan said. Then they could put a trace on it. Try and get his location from the GPS.

A number of factors could hamper that, however. If Bill had a phone old enough it had no GPS. Or if he'd turned it off or taken the sim card out. But they had to try.

Declan prayed more. They were so close. So close to finding Anna, and to bringing in Bill. Close to ending the threat against him and Nicholas. He didn't want to walk away from Portia—not until he had the chance to find out if a relationship between them might work. And if she was willing to take the risk. He could take a few more days of vacation. Without the life-in-jeopardy danger.

Portia noted the phone number, and two ATF agents escorted Beth away. Despite the woman's protest at being arrested, Portia wasn't going to soften. "When I find my agent, I'll talk to the ATF. Tell them you cooperated."

Beth sputtered as she was taken out. They followed to the walkway and disembarked the ferry. Too bad they had to go back to Bremerton now to get to the office. It hadn't been a wasted trip, but were they farther from Anna now than they had been?

"Thanks, Squire. As soon as you can, please." She hung up her phone.

Declan had been so lost in his own thoughts he hadn't even realized she was on the phone.

The look on her face wasn't good, so he set his hand on her shoulder. "We'll get something. I have faith, and I'm believing and praying that Anna is going to be found. I'm standing on that."

"I don't know if I can do the same," Portia said. "I just keep wondering if we'll find her body somewhere. Like we found Frank Parsons."

Bill had shot Frank in order to draw out Declan and begin his plan of revenge on their family. He could very well do the same to Anna. Still, Declan was going to trust for the best outcome.

Declan touched her cheek. He leaned close to her. "Whatever happens, I'll be here with you. No matter what. We face this together."

Portia took a deep breath. "Together."

He nodded, then leaned closer. Slowly, so she could pull away if she didn't want this to happen. But she didn't. Declan's lips met hers. He kept the kiss short because of the people around them, going about their day. Attention wasn't what this was about.

When he pulled back, a smile tugged at Portia's lips. In his pocket, Declan's phone buzzed. He pulled it out.

She said, "I'm going to check in with ATF about the

man Beth met with. Maybe then we'll have heard from Squire."

Declan nodded and read the text message that had just come in.

It listed an address, a rest stop on the highway.

Two p.m. Come alone, and I'll tell NCIS where they can find the redhead.

This was their chance to get Anna back. His chance. Declan glanced once at the spot where Portia chatted with an ATF agent.

And then he disappeared into the crowd.

EIGHTEEN

Portia had tracked Declan's progress using the GPS locator on his phone from the minute she'd realized he had ditched her. Thanks to Squire getting her the link, she knew exactly where he was. The cab he'd flagged down had taken him to Sea-Tac Airport, where he'd rented a car.

She also knew thanks to Squire that Bill had told Declan to meet him at a parking lot in Tiger Mountain State Forest. To have given him that location, along with the two-hour time limit, Bill must have known where they were. How, she didn't know. But it would seem that he did because he'd given Declan time to get to the state forest, east of Seattle, to make the deadline. If they'd been at the office, they would never have made it.

Portia pulled over to the side of the highway at a lookout spot. This state park was beautiful, but she couldn't enjoy it right now. Not when both Declan's and Anna's lives were at stake.

It was definitely Bill who had contacted Declan. Squire had hacked Bill's phone fast enough to see the message get sent before the phone was switched off again and his GPS disappeared. That had given him a springboard into Declan's phone. Portia didn't like the idea that she was essentially spying on him, but what did he expect? He'd gone off, half-cocked…to do what?

Save all their lives.

She stared at the blinking dot on the map that designated his car, one mile up the road at the parking lot where Bill had told him to be. Thirty-two minutes until "go" time. Declan was absolutely the kind of man who would put himself in harm's way just to save her team member. He didn't even know Anna that well, and yet he'd give up his freedom. His life. Just to force Bill to keep up his end of the bargain and set Anna free.

Anything Portia did now to intervene would jeopardize their safety. Her hands were tied. For now, she had to hang back. Trust that Declan could get Anna for her. That he would keep himself safe until she got to him.

Before she lost him for good.

Portia swiped to her call history and tapped his name. She watched the trees sway with a gentle breeze while the dial tone echoed through the car speakers.

"Hey."

At least he had the decency to sound guilty.

"Hey yourself."

"I'm sorry I ditched you." His voice was gentle.

Portia didn't want to soften but could feel exactly that happening. She steeled herself against it. "It was a dumb thing to do." She scrunched up her mouth because he couldn't see it, and said, "But I understand why you did."

Because she'd have done the same thing.

The note had said, "Come alone." Neither of them would have risked doing otherwise.

"I'll get Anna back."

For her. He didn't say it, but Portia could hear the words in the silence. "I know you will. That's not the point, is it?" This was tearing open old wounds Portia had preferred to keep buried. Bandaged as best she could but covered up. Like the wound on her temple. Hidden, but she could still feel it.

She gritted her teeth. "And you?" Did she want to hear that he was prepared to give his life, to allow Bill to kill him? She bit her lip. "What about you?"

Declan was silent. "You know, Portia."

She knew he'd give his life. And she would be alone. Again. "I know you had better do everything you can to stay alive until I get there. That's what I know. It'll take me a couple of minutes, but I'll come as fast as I can. Bill won't get far with you before we take him down."

"How far behind me are you?"

"About a mile."

"Seriously?" Declan said. "How did you know where I went?"

"Squire hacked Bill's phone. He saw the text you received. I have your GPS location."

"Ah."

"I guess you figured you'd have a longer head start than that, huh?"

He said, "Thank you for coming anyway."

"You think I wouldn't have your back? Or that I wouldn't do it in a way that doesn't violate his instructions?"

"So who has your back?"

"ATF is tied up. I put a call out, so I have agents on their way. We have time before the deadline for them to get here."

"That's what I'm used to from the Secret Service." He paused a second. "I guess I've never had it from someone I...cared about before."

Portia rubbed her hand down her leg, toward her knee. The pushing motion relieved some tension.

He said, "What is it?"

"I don't want to lose anyone else. I don't want to have to do this alone." She sucked in a choppy breath. "Without the people *I* care about."

"Your father?"

A sheen of tears blurred the trees in front of her. She blinked against the rush of emotion.

"You told me he was sick," Declan said. "And then you told Eric he committed suicide."

"Both are true." She choked the words out, wishing he was here with her, but at the same time glad she was alone. Would it be easier to tell him if she didn't have to look in his face and see the knowledge of how badly she'd failed? Either way he would know.

Portia said, "It was cancer. They gave him weeks. He could barely walk by then, but he wanted to go fishing." She cleared her throat. "One last time, he said." A single tear rolled down her cheek. She swiped it away. "So I took him out. It was cloudy. The waves were choppy, but he wanted to go out on the ocean. 'Catch me a big one,' he said."

"Portia." Her name was a groan from his lips.

"I'd set him up on a deck chair. Blanket on his lap. Gloves to hold his fishing pole. He told me to grab him some more coffee from below deck. Said he was still cold." She swiped at yet more tears on her cheeks, sniffed and said, "When I came back up the wheelchair was on its side. He must've been able to take a few steps, because he—"

Her voice dissolved into a series of sobs.

"He jumped overboard?"

"I never even heard the splash."

He'd never told her what he was going to do. Never once explained that he wanted to end his life like that.

Yes, she'd have tried to talk him out of it. But in the end, it had been his decision. And he'd never even trusted her with the chance to understand. To respect it.

He'd simply had her take him out on the boat—*used her* to get him there—and the minute her back was turned had left her.

Completely alone on the water.

"He didn't trust me. That's all I can think. He didn't believe I could handle it, and yet he left me to pick up the pieces afterward. To answer all the Coast Guard's questions when I told them where he went. To deal with all the legal stuff with his will, when there was no body. Did he know how many sideways looks I was going to get? People wondering if I'd pushed him over. Like I could claim his life insurance after that."

"Portia—"

"He didn't think about that, did he? And I'm supposed to not be mad at him? Well, I am. And he's dead, so what's the point of that? I don't win, whatever I do with it."

"Portia, hang on for a second."

She realized where he was, and what they were expecting. "Is it Bill? Is he there?"

"It isn't Bill."

"Oh, well, that's good—"

Portia's car door was opened from the outside.

She looked up at the person standing there and gasped.

The phone beeped on Declan's end, as though Portia had hung up. He was already half out of his car. He watched a woman with a limp to her stride make her way to him. That red hair.

Her clothes were dirty, her face streaked down one side with dried blood.

"Anna?"

Her head moved like she didn't know where to focus. Kind of like Declan's thoughts. He shut the car door and met her halfway. She had some visible injuries. Her breath came fast, and her gaze darted around.

But Declan still wanted to know why that conversation with Portia had ended so abruptly. Why had she hung up on him? He pushed aside the thought and focused on what was right in front of him. "Anna."

A moan pushed its way out of her throat. "Portia."

"What about her?"

He waited for her answer, wondering if she was simply wanting her friend. Or was it something else? When she said nothing, he said, "Is Portia in danger?"

"Portia..." She shook her head.

Declan went back to his car and retrieved his cell phone. While he listened to it ring on Portia's end, he wandered back to Anna. "Do you need an ambulance?"

She shook her head. "It's just bruises apart from this." She motioned to the cut on her temple, which had long since stopped bleeding. Bill must have coldcocked her with his gun. He knew from experience that hurt like nobody's business.

"Anything else?" he asked her, the phone against his ear still ringing on the other end.

"Is Chris okay? You found him, right?"

Declan nodded. "He's in the hospital. He'll be fine."

Relief washed over her face.

"How did you get away?"

"Bill parked not far from here. He's been working with United American Citizens this whole time."

Declan nodded. "We know that. He wanted to meet me here, trade me for you."

She frowned. "No, I don't think that was it."

"What do you mean?"

"He wants to draw you out and kill you, but UAC is breathing down his neck. I heard him on the phone." She paused, and her face turned assessing. Like she was processing what she'd seen and heard. "I think they want him to take care of Portia. To kill her."

"How will that help?" If Portia was in danger, he had to get Anna in the car and get to her. Now.

"To slow down the ATF, and all the other feds. Murder one of their own and get everyone tied up with the investigation."

He said, "That will only make them come at UAC that much harder. To take them down for what was done to 'one of their own.'"

"I think they plan to strike before then. To hit their target while the feds are scrambling."

Maybe. Declan couldn't figure how the man would suddenly change his mind—or take orders instead of doing his own thing. He'd been after Declan. But was he more scared of UAC than he was determined to kill Declan? He'd followed that MO in sending the text. Had it been a ruse? Make them all think he was still after Declan, while in fact he was now more interested in doing UAC's bidding—for whatever reason?

Maybe Anna was confused after everything she'd been through. It might take hours to unscramble everything she needed to tell him.

But he didn't have hours.

And Portia wasn't picking up.

"Tell me how you got away?" he asked.

"He was looking at his phone. Muttering, and grumbling about orders." She sucked in a short breath. "I took advantage of his distraction and just ran. He yelled a bit, and fired a shot after me, but didn't follow. I kept going, praying I'd run into someone so I could call for help."

He thanked God then that she'd run into him and not someone else. Getting help would have taken longer.

Declan ended the call to Portia before he was asked to leave a voice mail and called the NCIS office. He asked the person who answered the call to have the agents assisting Portia get to her location as soon as possible. After a few seconds on hold, the agent came back.

"They're ten minutes out."

"Tell them to hurry." Declan hung up. Ten minutes could mean the difference between life and death for her. "Let's go." He motioned Anna to the car.

Portia's phone lay discarded on the ground. Shattered. The screen had gone dark a minute ago. Surely whoever had called her would know to send help. At least, she hoped so.

"I said, get out of the car."

She stared at Bill, one leg out of the car already. Hands up so he could see her palms, she folded out of the car slowly. Trying to buy herself even more time.

He'd come here, instead of going after Declan. That didn't make sense. But regardless, he was here. And pointing a gun at her. There was no time to figure out the why of him showing up where she was instead of in the location where Declan was told to wait.

And where was her backup?

"Keep your hands up." He took two steps to the left. Reached out for her gun.

He thought he was going to disarm her? Portia kept the fearful look on her face as he moved toward her weapon.

In one move she grabbed the hand reaching for her gun and the hand holding his own weapon. With a grip on both, she held them spread wide.

And headbutted him.

Bill roared.

Portia seconded the sentiment. Headbutting hurt about equally with being the one who got headbutted. But she couldn't let it distract her. She let go of his empty hand and grasped the one holding the gun with both.

They wrestled for the gun. She lost her footing and they both fell. She landed on her back, Bill on top of her. Portia immediately rolled, not wanting to be in a disadvantaged position. But Bill caught her chin with his elbow.

She hissed, blinking away stars.

Then the gun went off.

NINETEEN

Portia cried out. She heard an engine rev, even as her phone lit up and started to ring again. The influx of noise was overwhelming. But it disappeared as a roaring sound eclipsed everything else. Adrenaline. Her own breath. Every rapid beat of her heart.

"Drop the gun!" Declan's words penetrated the rush in her ears.

Bill grabbed her arm and pulled her up. She screamed at the pain of him squeezing the gunshot wound in her arm. The one he'd given her only seconds before. She scrambled to get her feet under her and stood, her head swimming.

Bill pulled her in front of him. "You drop yours. Or she's dead." He pressed the gun against her temple, his body angled so she couldn't get a grip on her gun.

"Declan."

He ignored her and climbed out of the car, his gun aimed on Bill. Could he get off that shot without hurting her? She trusted him. He was here. Her life was in danger, and he'd come to help. *God, help his aim be true.*

Bill dragged her back two steps. "Gun down, Harris."

"That isn't my name."

"Why doesn't Declan lower his gun, and you can lower yours," Portia suggested. "And you just go."

This battle of wills wasn't worth any of them getting hurt. That was the last thing she wanted.

"Just leave, Bill."

"And give up this prime opportunity to kill both of you?" He laughed, the sound grating against her ears.

Where was their backup? Surely the other feds would be here any second, right? They were supposed to be meeting her here, but she didn't know how much time there was before Bill's deadline from the text. That was moot now, but still. The feds were cutting it close.

So close it could cost a life.

"I'm not putting my gun down." The look Declan shot her was stone-cold. Because he didn't want to be vulnerable? She didn't figure he was more determined to protect himself than he was to keep Portia—and Anna—safe.

Beyond him, Anna sat in the passenger seat of Declan's vehicle.

The reality that her colleague and friend was all right washed over her, and her knees wobbled. Threatened to collapse. *Thank You, God. Help us now.* They still needed Him. So badly. She always would—danger or no.

The roar of car engines approaching caught her attention. Bill stiffened. He'd noticed. Portia figured it was her backup.

"Go now," she said. "And there's a chance for you to live free."

Except not, since he'd be hunted until he was caught and then jailed.

Bill shifted. Her car was closer than Declan's rental. As the vehicles closed in, Bill shoved her. He dived for her car and landed half in the passenger door she'd left open. Portia landed on her injured shoulder and cried out. Black filled her vision for a second before she turned to a sitting position, fighting to get her gun up.

Declan took cover and fired off three shots. Bill hit the gas. Declan kept firing, hitting the hood. Then the side right by one of the tires. She glanced past him to see multiple cars pull into the lot.

Bill spun the car in an arc and sped off. Still sitting on the ground, she lifted her own gun and fired. The bullet slammed the back of the car as it drove away. Then another in the side panel. Bill roared out of the parking lot in a spray of gravel.

Two cars that had just pulled into the lot peeled off to follow him.

"Portia!" Declan ran over. "You okay?"

Portia nodded and let him help her to her feet. "Anna."

Declan made sure she had her footing, then stepped out of the way. Portia moved to her colleague, who had opened the passenger door but hadn't gotten out. She crouched. "You all right?"

"Yeah, boss." Anna nodded.

Portia didn't want the woman to put on a brave face just for her. "Seems like we could both use an ambulance." She smiled, but Anna didn't return it.

The agents who'd also showed up were out of their cars. A map had been spread across the hood of one of the vehicles and a conference was being held. There was a lot of hand gesturing and talking on phones.

Portia wanted to go over and insert herself into whatever manhunt was happening. She wanted to find Bill and prayed those in pursuit would capture him. But for right now, Anna being safe and cared for was more important. Not to mention, her arm hurt like no one's business, and the adrenaline was dissipating. It left her shaky enough she couldn't crouch anymore.

So she stood. Locked her knees. "Declan, can I use your phone?"

He had her broken one up off the ground. He came over, holding out his cell. She called in to the director and asked to be kept in the loop about the search for Bill. She also asked for an ambulance.

"We should go after Bill." Anna stood up. The hand on the roof of the car to steady her took something away from her attempt to look strong and capable. She was, just not after she'd been through a kidnapping ordeal.

"You aren't going anywhere," Portia said. Declan looked like he agreed with her, giving Portia the same glance he gave Anna. Like he wanted both of them to sit down.

"She's right," he said. "They'll get Bill. Our priority is being safe and staying that way."

"He hurt Chris. He took me." Anna gasped. "He was going to kill both of you. And he's involved with UAC. We have to stop him." Her face paled.

Portia moved first, but Declan got there quicker. *Thank You, God.* Declan was here to help.

The man she loved.

Declan caught Anna before she slumped to the ground and laid her down gently. Portia and Anna were alive. He'd imagined the worst and was more than relieved to know Portia was okay. Though that wound on her arm looked nasty and needed medical attention.

Declan could hardly believe they'd come through this. He thought for sure one of them would be dead now. But then, he'd also believed Bill would be caught. Now instead the man was in the wind. And who knew where he would go? Declan had no idea what the license plate number was on Portia's car, or if it had any kind of anti-theft system.

At least they had Anna back now, though by the look of her she'd been completely overwhelmed by the experience to the point her mind and body had given up and she'd passed out from the stress.

Declan said, "You okay?"

Portia said nothing. She crouched beside them, wincing at whatever injuries she had aside from that nasty wound on her upper shoulder. There had been something there on her face, right before Anna collapsed. He wanted to ask her about it.

A fed came over, carrying a first-aid kit.

Portia spoke then. "She needs looking at."

He gave her a pointed look. "They both do."

"I'm fine with going second." She shifted her arm, then said, "He only winged me."

Declan didn't miss the wince. While the guy worked on Anna, he waved her aside. Before he could speak she leaned in, her face to his shirt. He put his arms around her in a loose hug, careful not to put pressure on her wound. Or any of his. He wanted to kiss her.

"You're okay?" Portia looked and sounded exhausted now.

"I was going to ask the same about you." He pushed aside all thoughts of kissing her, focusing on now. This wasn't over. As much as he had wanted it to be—and had assumed that it would be—Bill was still out there.

But Anna was here.

Not a full victory, but they had won this battle.

"Agents are in pursuit of Bill." He said it as much for her benefit as his. It wasn't news to either of them. "And an ambulance will be on its way."

"I know." She nodded, her face still against his chest. So much strength wrapped in someone with an ability to admit to weakness when the time was right.

She put on a brave face, but then showed Declan that she needed him.

A paradox he wasn't sure he would ever understand. Though he seriously appreciated it. Bravado got boring.

Declan kissed her forehead then. "We got her back."

Portia nodded.

"She'll heal, and we *will* find Bill. Life will go back to normal."

But was that really what he wanted? To go back to Washington, DC, and move on from all this, knowing she was here doing the same?

Now that Portia was in his world, Declan couldn't help thinking he might not want things to go back to the way they used to be. Life on the East Coast was full, but not fulfilling. His job no longer presented the challenge it used to.

Could he move? Change everything about his life, just for a shot at a relationship?

He was going to have to pray about that.

Perhaps a career change would be good for him. Declan figured he didn't have the temperament for investigations work. Something in private protection, maybe. There had to be a market for his skill set. He'd have to look into it—considering he wanted a job where he had time to make regular trips to California to see his brother. And his friends, Grady and Skylar.

Soon enough the ambulance arrived, and Anna was loaded inside. Portia pulled away and glanced at him. "There's a lot going on in that head of yours."

Declan said, "You go, as well. I'll meet you at the hospital."

She bit her lip. Looked once at where Anna was being secured in the back of the ambulance so they could leave. Then she looked back at Declan.

He wrapped his arms around her again. "Bill might

be in the wind, but this isn't over. We'll find him, and we'll take him down."

"I know."

He leaned back, arms still around her waist, and looked down at her. Shock had rippled through him at the idea she was dead—or hurt. He'd been overwhelmed by fear.

Portia frowned. "What is it?"

"I'm just really glad you're all right."

She smiled, a sweet intimate look just for him. Declan wanted those every day of his life. Maybe they should just find a way to make it work. What was the alternative? Loneliness?

His phone rang, a number he didn't recognize. Declan showed her the display.

"That's an NCIS cell number."

They had to have a series of numbers allocated to them for her to know that. Secret Service did the same. He swiped to answer the call while a new surge of excitement rushed through him at the idea they might not have lost Bill for good. Though the idea of Portia going after the man with a gunshot wound in her arm didn't sit right with him.

He put the call on speaker. "This is Agent Stringer."

"We lost him," the caller said. "Bill Frawley got away."

Declan didn't answer, he just hung up. Out of hope. He couldn't even tell Portia they'd catch him eventually. Would they? Maybe he would be forced to live the rest of his life with a target on his back.

And Portia would have to do the same.

Unless he found Bill.

Portia said, "You have this look on your face. Like you have something to say, and I'm not going to like it."

Declan decided she'd more than not like it if he asked

her to sit this one out. Instead of going there, he said, "I just want you to get your arm checked out. It's probably hurting a whole lot."

Her gaze flicked to something over his shoulder. She nodded.

Declan heard the door to the ambulance shut. The engine revved and he turned in time to see it pull away. "You don't..."

"Anna needs medical attention. My part comes when she wakes up and needs a friend. So I think you should drive me to the hospital." She lifted her chin, a gleam in her gaze. "Unless you have something better to do?"

He surveyed the area, then held out his hand to her even though it was only a few steps to his car. "Let's go."

"You're doing that Secret Service thing, protecting me."

It was a habit, but he didn't want to tell her that. The truth was so much more. She took his hand and let him steady her as she got in the passenger side. Her face paled, the pain growing. She'd lost a good amount of blood.

And yet, she'd chosen to go with him instead of in the ambulance with her friend.

Declan got her settled in the front seat of his car, where she leaned back and shut her eyes. If she hadn't opted to come, he'd have been alone.

As he rounded the vehicle, it occurred to him that Bill might have circled back. The gun he had was out of bullets, but a car could be used as a weapon. Declan scanned the area but didn't see Portia's car anywhere.

Declan got in the driver's side and started the engine. Determination surged in him.

This needed to be over. Now.

He was going to make sure Bill was caught.

TWENTY

"I think the bleeding slowed down."

Declan looked up from where he was bent over her arm, applying over-the-counter antibacterial cream to the wound on her arm. He didn't look impressed.

"Well, it has."

He'd stopped at a chain pharmacy and picked up a basketful of medical supplies, along with a few things like energy bars and bottled orange juice. Portia hadn't woken up until he got back in the car with two grocery bags full of stuff.

That split second when she realized she'd been alone for those few minutes had rushed through her like an icy ocean breeze. The same breeze she'd felt when she emerged from below deck to realize her father was gone.

Okay, so logically she knew it wasn't the *same* breeze. But, still. The feeling was the same.

Declan covered the wound, and then wrapped a bandage over it. She gritted her teeth so he didn't know how much that hurt.

"Sorry, it has to be kinda tight."

Portia nodded, feeling the prick of tears in the corners of her eyes and the way her nose stung.

"I got you a sling for your arm, to take the weight off it."

Great. She didn't want to wear one of those. Yes, it would help. Did she want to be the cop with her arm in a sling? Not so much.

"Thanks."

Declan chuckled. "Yeah, you looked super excited about it."

Portia smiled. "Thank you."

"You said that."

The smile curled her lips farther up. Declan leaned over and pressed lips to hers. "Sorry."

"I'm not complaining."

"You just looked so cute. I couldn't resist."

"Don't tell anyone else you think I'm cute," she said. "I'll never live it down."

Declan chuckled. "Are you light-headed?" He touched her forehead with the back of his hand.

Portia waved him away. "I'm fine." The pain meds he'd also gotten her were helping. She likely needed something stronger, but at least she hadn't required stitches. It was a graze at best. Yes, a graze from a bullet, but still a graze. Slight burns from the heated metal and something a lot like road rash in a tiny line.

She would heal.

"I'm glad you're okay. I wouldn't want this to be a delirium thing where you won't remember it after you've slept."

Portia said, "I guess I'm just…used to you now." He frowned, so she added, "As opposed to being alone, miserable and afraid to let anyone in since my dad left me the way that he did." It was more than she'd intended to say, but now it was out she didn't regret it.

She turned her broken phone over and over on her thigh.

"Thank you for telling me about him." Declan touched

her cheek and she glanced up from her phone at him. "Thank you for trusting me with that story."

She nodded. It was hard to be strong all the time. Yes, she was naturally independent. She'd earned her spot as the NCIS team leader in a male-dominated field by working to be better and stronger than all the men she'd beaten out to get to this spot. There was no way she could break. They'd all know she wasn't as self-assured as she pretended to be.

Was anyone?

"I know about your family. It seemed right to tell you about mine." Portia gave him a small smile. "After all, isn't that part of getting to know each other? You know about my dad, and about Steve. There isn't much else to tell." She shrugged the shoulder not in a sling and said, "There's my apartment, which you've been to, and I have a tiny house on the beach near La Push. That's all of it."

Declan said, "Let's see. I have a condo in Virginia I'm hardly ever at except to shower and change clothes. I paddleboard as often as I can, and for some reason I really hate cheese. Like, with a passion."

Portia laughed. Before she could ask him about the paddleboarding, his phone rang. Declan put the call on speaker and said, "Squire. What do you have for us?"

"We got a result back on the BOLO the feds put out on your car being driven by a man with Bill's description. He took the highway southwest, and now he's on the five freeway."

Declan pulled out of the pharmacy parking lot and headed for the same freeway. "Any idea where he's headed?"

Another voice came on. "It's Lenny. You okay, Portia?"

"I'm good," Portia said. "What've you got?"

"I talked with ATF about the intel they got from Beth, Eric and Mallory. Between the three of them, Steve learned where their compound was located. Beth didn't know what they had planned, and neither Eric nor Mallory gave up the information." Lenny took a breath, then continued, "Regardless, he put together a team. They raided the compound an hour ago. Six members of United American Citizens were arrested. Four more are at-large in the forest around the compound and agents are tracking them."

"And Bill?" Portia asked.

Squire said, "From the direction he's headed, I'd say he's going there. Probably to get firepower. Maybe to regroup in a friendly place that's essentially off the grid." He sounded almost excited at the prospect of being integral in the takedown of a suspect. "So right now the feds are tearing apart the whole place, impounding all the weapons and any papers or computers they might find, and they're spread through the surrounding forests with dogs rounding up the rest."

Portia said, "Bill's going to see them as he makes his approach. There's no way he won't realize the place is crawling with feds." She tapped the broken phone against her leg some more. "So how do we lay this trap down?"

"Steve said he can pull his people back. Get all the vehicles moved inside UAC barns and have everyone remain out of sight as he makes his approach. Bill might not completely fall for it, but Steve thinks he'll get close enough ATF can simply snap the trap shut."

"On *our* suspect?" She didn't exactly like the fact they were going to get her man but supposed that if they were already there then she could simply take custody of Bill when they arrived. Not to mention the tiny problem of her injury. And Declan wasn't a hundred percent either.

Squire chuckled. Even Declan shot her a look. Squire said, "I'm sure they'll hold him until you get there."

"If they don't give away the fact they're there and spook Bill so he runs."

"If they do, we'll just keep searching for him."

Portia ran down all the variables in her head. "How long until Bill gets there?"

There was quiet for a second, and Squire said, "Fifty-two minutes. Give or take."

"What about Declan and I?"

"An hour ten."

She pressed her lips together.

Declan said, "Tell ATF to secure Bill and hold him until we get there."

"Yes, sir."

Squire hung up before she could say anything.

"Problem?"

Portia shook her head, disbelieving. Was this what being a team, the two of them, meant? Declan was strong, and in command. She was, as well. Would they butt heads all the time, both wanting to be in leadership? She hoped not.

He reached over and squeezed her leg. "I promise I'll let you do the actual arresting."

"Great. You do the victim-not-getting-hurt thing, and I'll do my *job*." Sarcasm laced her tone, but she didn't back down. Or apologize. Her arm hurt, and he had to know exactly what he was getting into.

Declan let out a deep belly laugh. "Don't worry, I remember the balance of how this goes. After all, you've been saving my life all week."

"You better believe I have."

Yet again he'd matched her. Strength for strength, just like he had all week. Portia glanced out the window and smiled. Partners. Equals. She couldn't help feeling like, despite the tendency for their dominant personalities to conflict, they were perfectly matched.

The way only God could bring two people together.

Declan looked out over the driveway of this compound, where the group had been holed up. The central building looked like a huge log cabin and was surrounded by outbuildings in varying degrees of run-down.

Agents roamed the whole area, most in vests and carrying rifles. They both accepted a vest with ATF emblazoned on it, even though he had one under his shirt. In this type of situation, he had to look like the fed he was, if only to avoid being mistaken for a possible suspect.

Portia pulled a jacket from the trunk of his car and slid it over her arm. Declan helped get it over her shoulder, not liking at all that she'd taken off the sling for now.

Steve strode over, clearly the commanding agent on the takedown. "I have more agents on the way, as well as my director. We're still running down four of their men."

Portia shifted, not giving away to the man the fact she'd been injured. "Any sign of Bill?"

Declan was as proud of her for her strength as he was frustrated she felt like it was necessary to put up a front. She would do her job to the detriment of her health, and was he going to have to put up with it? Maybe he could convince her to take better care of herself. Maybe he should let her do what she wanted and support her.

And maybe the balance between those two things was something he would be juggling for the rest of his life.

Steve said, "The agents I have running the UAV from the office have aerial footage of an abandoned vehicle that fits the description you gave us. I sent two agents to check it out. Seems like he ditched his car a mile east of here, probably intending to approach on foot. What he was planning to do from there is anyone's guess."

Portia said, "You don't think he's in good standing?" Squire hadn't been able to locate him for the last half hour. Was he really here?

"The couple of UAC guys that talked before we got them loaded up in the van figure Bill and his brother sold them out. They'd probably kill him on sight at this point."

Declan's hand never strayed far from his weapon, knowing this situation would likely get sticky at any moment. One of the men the ATF was after could break free and get a weapon, or Bill could come gunning for him.

He turned to Portia. "I don't suppose you'd be content to stay here, with the ATF, and let me do this?"

She kept her steady gaze on him.

Steve muttered something and wandered off, chuckling quietly. Declan didn't need the man's opinion. It was worth a try, at least. "Want to start with the car, work back from there?"

She nodded. "Let's go."

Badges on display, they hiked the mile to the car. As they drew close to it, Declan said, "That's—"

"My car." She sounded mad, and he didn't blame her.

The driver's door was open, the dome light on inside. Declan scanned the area, then ducked his head in and looked around. "I don't see Bill anywhere."

"Me either," she said.

"I guess easy was too much to ask."

The corner of Portia's mouth curled up as she walked to the rear of the car, where he could no longer see the humor on her face. He knew what she was looking for—the two ATF agents who'd been sent to check out the car.

"Any sign of them?" he asked. If they hadn't reached the

car before Portia and Declan, then they'd either run into another issue before they got to it. Or Bill had found them.

Portia pulled up short, her eyes on the ground. "Declan."

He trotted over, pulling his weapon from its holster. "What is..."

Two bodies on the ground. Vests, no protection against this threat. ATF badges—which hadn't stopped Bill from shooting them each in the head.

Sightless eyes stared back at him.

Lord, help us. The man was a serious threat if he'd bested two agents quickly enough he'd killed both before they could react. One man could be surprised, but the second would have had time to respond. Surely.

Not this time.

Declan set his free hand on her shoulder. "Let's go back to the compound."

She nodded, and they got moving. There was no way to track Bill. He'd proved himself a formidable threat. Declan and Portia had to keep their eyes open. Even more than they had been so far. Those two ATF agents had been trained to face threats like this, and Bill had killed them.

They both scanned as they walked. Still, Declan could hear nothing but trees. Rustling—the breeze, and what animals hadn't scattered when armed agents in boots started tromping through their land.

Declan couldn't stop the swirl of thoughts. "If Bill killed those two agents, why didn't he just get back in the car and drive away?"

"He had a different plan?"

"I guess. Doesn't make sense, though, if he knew there were feds here."

"I didn't say the plan would make sense," Portia said, a rueful smile on her face. "They don't usually, and he's flipped the situation on us once today already. You know how people can get ideas in their heads, and if they're strong-willed enough they can justify anything to themselves. Even to the point that the most ridiculous idea seems to them like it would be foolproof."

"And they think it's just misunderstood genius, is that it?"

"Or he's on something," Portia said. "Maybe he's running on chemical impulses, determined to do whatever he has in his head."

"Help one of the UAC guys, maybe? Like his son-in-law?"

She shrugged her good shoulder. "I guess we'll find out."

"Or we'll catch him and ask him ourselves."

Portia shot him a dark look. Worried. She didn't think they were going to catch Bill? Or maybe she wasn't convinced they would survive it if they did. Both of them were a little banged up.

Declan thought of those two agents, ATF guys just here to do their jobs. Now they were dead, and their families would have to learn what it was like to live their lives without those loved ones. Declan didn't want to know what it was like to live without his brother. That drive had brought him here.

It had brought him to Portia.

"Whatever happens," he said. "This is something we're going to face together."

She bit her lip, her gaze on the terrain around them.

Bill could be hiding behind any one of those trees.

"Portia?"

Her gaze locked to the northwest of where they stood. Her lips parted, but he was already reacting. All the training he'd had surged to a point where he'd never been more determined to save someone's life. Not ever before.

Declan dived. His arm slid around Portia and he twisted his body, taking hers with it. Gun hand still outstretched, he landed on his back as the first shots rang out through the forest.

They both grunted, Portia's cry full of pain. His wasn't much better. But he couldn't help that. Declan rolled as the gunshots kept coming. Blast after blast, after blast. The bruise on his chest burned like fire. He hauled Portia up to a low crouch and they scurried through the trees. They needed cover—a position they could be protected enough in to fight back.

Hot fire slammed into his thigh and Declan fell to the ground with a cry.

TWENTY-ONE

Declan hit the ground, his weight tugging her down beside him. He grunted, the feeling reverberating from him through her arm. It spasmed, probably not in sympathy for his leg. But she was ignoring the pain from her wound. "Come on." She tugged at his arms. "We can't stay in the open. He'll pick us off."

The shots had stopped. Where was Bill? She didn't like the idea that he was regrouping. Maybe switching out rifle magazines? He'd probably grabbed a gun from one of those ATF agents he'd killed. How many rounds did he have?

Would he keep shooting, and shooting, until they were dead?

They traversed two feet, which felt like a mile. Declan twisted around and leaned against a tree. He still had his gun. Good. The wound on his leg was distinctly *not* good.

They needed help.

She transferred her gun to her off hand. Her shoulder smarted like she couldn't have imagined it would, but she'd shoot if she had to.

Declan scanned the area behind her while she pulled out her phone. Despite the fact the screen was shattered, she managed to dial Steve's number. Not thinking too much about the fact they needed his help. Another broken phone. How much longer would it even work?

He answered quickly. "Mason."

"We're taking fire."

"That was you? We heard. I have agents on the way."

"The two you sent to the car are dead."

"Copy that." He was breathing hard, moving fast. She didn't want to rely on him, but Declan was hurt.

Tears filled her eyes at the idea of being left alone. Again.

Declan touched her cheek. The warmth in his palm settled her nerves, though he didn't look at her. He was keeping watch to make sure Bill didn't sneak up on them. And she was doing the same behind him. Between the two of them, they had all three hundred sixty degrees covered. Ready to face Bill as a team.

"We'll be there ASAP." Steve hung up.

Portia tossed the phone on the ground.

Bill could take them out before the ATF even got there. That was the last thing she wanted when she'd just found Declan. Or he'd found her. She didn't know which way around that was. Things had been out of control the past few days. Now they were both hurt, and the suspect was still out there.

"You think he ran?"

Portia shook her head.

"What are we going to do?"

She knew what she was going to do. Portia stood. She presented more of a target, but without narrowing down on Bill's position this would never work. The shots had come from behind them. She scanned the terrain, looking for the glint of a rifle. Listening for the snick of a magazine being loaded. The ratchet of the gun as it was readied to fire. Listening for footsteps as Bill made his way closer.

With an ATF rifle, Bill could pick them off from behind a spot where he had the kind of coverage she'd never be able to see him. Even in the daylight.

Lord, help me. She needed His help if she was going to spot Bill. If she was going to be attuned enough to the landscape that she would have any hope of seeing him. Her skills and training would only take her so far. If Bill was going to be caught they would need God's protection to keep from being hurt any more than they were.

"Portia." Declan said her name like a warning. A caution for her to be careful, and an expression of how worried he was. He knew the threat here. They could be picked off at any moment. Dead like those two ATF agents.

She crouched, close enough she and Declan were practically nose to nose. There wasn't time enough to say everything she wanted to.

She waited long enough for him to ask, "What is it?" A crinkle shifted in his brow.

She said, "I love you."

He opened his mouth to reply, but she didn't let him.

"I just wanted you to know that." Before she left him, and maybe didn't come back at all. Like her father.

She didn't know if a relationship between them was going to work, but she had to do something. Get the upper hand, somehow.

She straightened. "Stay here." Like he was going anywhere.

"Portia." He hissed her name, but she didn't turn back.

Portia raced between trees and over a fallen log, through the forest. She angled her steps so that she moved in an arc. Trying her best to keep her footsteps as quiet as possible, she moved as quickly as she could. *God, please let this work.*

Her idea counted on Bill seeing Declan alone, and exposing his position to her without realizing. She didn't need him to close in on Declan. And she wanted to believe she didn't need him to take a shot she could trace back to its origin point.

God, help me see his location.

She knew the general area. As she made her way, she looked for those telltale signs. She prayed she would see him before he saw her. That she would catch him. That Declan would live.

There.

She saw him move. His blue jacket, between the trees. She prayed he would come quietly. She also prayed Steve and his guys would get here. Even though, emotionally, she no longer had—or wanted—a connection with him. That part of her life was over. But she still needed the ATF to back her up in this.

Portia fully intended to thank God for the bigger blessing that He had given her.

Declan.

Whether he felt the same way or not. Whether they could work out a future together or not. Whatever happened, she was glad he knew now how she felt.

Portia stepped on a dry branch. The crack echoed through the forest and she froze. Gun ready. Heart still in that state of prayer she hadn't let go of…in days. For the first time she was seeking God fully. Relying on Him, knowing her own strength wasn't going to be enough. And that was okay. She could do a lot, but in the end what was the guarantee? Even her own heart had deceived her in the past. God wanted what was best for her, and she was going to rest in that.

As soon as Bill was in cuffs.

She took another step. Then another. Moving so she was closer to Bill.

She couldn't see Declan. Bill was blocking her view of him. She'd left him alone, the way her father had left her. She was going to have to ask him to forgive her for that. She understood now that sometimes leaving was best for the other person. Someone she loved. But only the kind of separation where she trusted God that they would only be separated for a short time.

And though she could never do what her father had done, she at least understood why. Her father hadn't wanted to burden her more than he had already. Hadn't wanted to lay the responsibility of his burial on her. Or the emotional turmoil of watching him deteriorate even more.

She forgave him then, in her heart, knowing he'd loved her. Portia let go of the bitterness she'd been feeling toward him. The unforgiveness. She released all of it right then. Planted her feet, and called out, "Bill. Drop the gun and put your hands on your head."

She had to trust Declan. Trust that he had his own gun aimed at Bill. Between the two of them, all the angles were covered. So long as Bill didn't try and kill Declan as his last resort.

"Bill Frawley!" Her voice boomed in the forest. "Drop your weapon."

He turned then and saw her behind him. Portia didn't get one single glimpse of Declan. *God, please let him be okay.* He hadn't spoken or fired a shot. Was he conscious? Maybe he'd passed out from his injury.

"Drop it. Now," she commanded.

His mouth curled into a sneer, but she wasn't intimidated. This man wasn't going to hurt any more of the people Portia cared about.

"Drop—"

He fired a shot.

She ducked, and heard it slam into a tree. She wasn't

faster than a bullet. Her arm stung from the strain of holding her gun tightly at shoulder height, but she had to keep it steady. Keep her aim true.

"Put it down, Bill." This was going to be his last warning.

He brought the gun up. Finger twitched. The shot came the same time the bullet left the barrel of her gun.

Her aim was true.

His bullet slammed into the tree beside her.

Shards of bark sprayed on her face.

Another shot came from behind her. Then one to her left. One to her right.

Multiple ATF agents shot Bill, taking him down. Once and for all. Eliminating the threat. The man who had killed two of their agents, shot Declan in the parking lot on base—she was sure of that now—and terrorized them all for days. The man who had kidnapped her teammates and hurt them.

The shots died down to silence.

Then the sounds of the forest reached her ears. The rustle of trees. The brush underfoot as agents made their way to the now dead man.

Portia sprinted past him, leaving Bill to the ATF. She rushed over to where Declan sat, face pale. Skin clammy. "I'll get you an ambulance. We'll get you out of here where they can patch you up."

His gun lay in his loose grip, by the side of his thigh. The not-bloody one. One eyebrow rose, and his eyes filled with humor. "Only if you come with me. See a doctor about your arm."

"I haven't forgotten about it." It hurt still, how would she have forgotten?

"Portia."

"Yes?" She crouched in front of him.

He motioned with his head for her to come closer.

She did. Close enough Declan pressed his lips to hers before he said, "I love you too."

She started to smile, immensely pleased he felt the same way. Realizing now that she'd actually been worried she felt that way when he didn't. After all, it had only been days since they'd met.

But the two of them, together? It felt so right. More right than anything in her life. Declan had healed something she'd known was broken but hadn't known how to fix.

She opened her mouth to say everything in her heart but didn't get the chance.

He said, "And don't ever do that again."

Declan winced as the nurse wrapped a bandage around his leg. Despite the meds, getting stitches had hurt a lot. The pull in his leg hadn't abated even now the bulk of it was over. All that was left was to get some crutches and fill the prescription.

As soon as Portia got here, and he apologized. He'd told her he loved her but then seconds later he'd told her never to leave him again. And while he really didn't want her fighting alone, she couldn't promise never to be in danger. It was a reality of her job that she had to face suspects. Even armed ones. She could potentially be in danger any day of the week.

It was Declan's own fear that had spoken. She knew what it was like to lose someone. He didn't want to face that same fear with her. And knew now that it wasn't her who had to fix that for him.

Declan had to trust God.

Only by relying on his heavenly father and being filled with His perfect love could Declan release the fear. He needed to walk in faith if he was going to not live a life full of strain and worry. Stress and distrust.

"All done." The nurse leaned back and stood, surveying his leg below where they'd cut off his pants so that one leg was shorts length.

"Thanks."

Portia stepped in just as the nurse headed out the door. The two smiled at each other, a polite greeting. Something in Portia's body language held her apart, her spine stiff. Her shoulders back—even with her arm in a sling. When she came to stand by his bed her face stayed blank. "I spoke with Steve. He said thanks to us both for all our help with this case, considering we assisted with Eric and Mallory. And we gave them Beth."

"Feels good we were able to provide intel they might not have gotten otherwise," he said. "And maybe even assisted in bringing down UAC before they did something terrible." That was the last thing any of them wanted, and they'd prevented them from hurting any innocent people. "Did he say what their plan was?"

Portia shook her head. "Just that they had blueprints for a couple of hospitals in the Seattle and Tacoma areas."

Declan whistled. "That's a huge amount of potential casualties right there."

"Steve also said that Samuel's father was taken in. Samuel has been placed with child services for now."

"That's good." Although, it was also a sad situation.

She nodded. "I'm glad the ATF managed to intervene on both counts."

Declan shifted to face her, dangling his legs off the side of the bed while at the same time trying to not look like an invalid.

She looked down at his leg and winced. "Anna's okay. She's actually kinda mad about the whole thing. She was more worried about what I was going to think about the fact she 'let Bill abduct them.'" Portia sighed. "I told her we'd talk about it when she was feeling better. I mean, it's not like it was her fault she got bested by him. We all did, really."

He nodded. "It might take time, but she'll get her head straight and realize it wasn't her fault. And I know you know that. But she will be okay."

She nodded. "It's just…fresh for her right now."

"Well, I'm okay, as you can see. And so are you." Reassurance was probably the name of the game here. Some comfort, not just to soften her up in the hope she'd react better when he apologized. But…maybe he could get her to relax a bit.

"How is your arm?" It was a start, but it wasn't what he wanted to say.

"It's sore. Probably not as sore as your leg, though." The slight softening in her face gave him hope.

"We're a pair of invalids, aren't we?" He smiled, trying to coax her to relax a bit more.

She smiled back. "I guess we shouldn't sign up for a triathlon anytime soon."

Declan chuckled. He held his hand out, palm up, and waited. Without too much hesitation she placed her hand in his and looked down at him. He looked up at her, not liking the disadvantaged position, but willing to stick with it considering it would help plead his case for him. Maybe it would help her feel sorry for him. To forgive him.

"I'm sorry for what I said."

She took a half step back, but he held on to her hand. "I…"

"It was wrong of me to put that on you." He really needed her to understand that his fear was just that. *His* fear. "I should never have—"

"It's okay." She tugged at his hand. "You don't have

to apologize for how you feel…" Her voice trailed off. What more was she going to say?

"I should, though. I care about you and I don't want you to be worried about how I'm going to react when you were just doing your job."

She frowned, the crinkle growing more pronounced, before it started to smooth out. "You care about me?"

"Of course I do." Didn't she know that? "I was being honest when I told you I loved you. It wasn't just pain, or the heat of the moment. And I wasn't just saying it because you did."

"Then what are you apologizing for?"

"Telling you not to leave like you did," he said. "Going off on your own, when I know that's what your job entails. I shouldn't have put that on you. Especially not considering…"

"My father?"

He nodded.

"I realized I need to forgive him." She looked aside. "He was doing what he thought was the best thing, the least upheaval for me. And I would have wanted that extra time with him, but I know he just didn't want to be a burden on me." She looked at him. "I realized I needed to let that pain go, and just simply grieve the loss. Not the how of it. Just the absence of him in my life." She paused. "I thought you were changing your mind about what you said… The other thing you said."

Declan tugged her closer to him so she stood between his knees, his hands on her waist. "I really do love you. I'm sorry you doubted that even for a second. The past few days have been…incredible. Stressful. Scary. Amazing."

She shook her head, a smile on her face. "That makes no sense at all."

"You don't agree?"

"I didn't say that."

He tugged her closer. "Yeah?"

"I meant it when I said I loved you. The past few days have been…all those things you said. Plus bullets flying, and chasing suspects." She shook her head and laughed.

"What?"

"We're doing this all wrong, aren't we? I told you I love you, and you've said the same. And that's great. But we haven't even gone on a date."

Declan said, "Given everything that's just happened I think we just crossed the six-month mark in relationship terms. After all, I've shared more meals, more stress and more life with you than any relationship I've had in a long time. At least from what I remember."

"I know what you mean."

He was glad she said that. Steve had been a part of things the last few days. And Declan knew their relationship was over. Still, his fragile male ego needed her to confirm again that things there were really done. Especially when this was so new—and, as this conversation confirmed, fragile, as well. He and Portia didn't need anything rocking the boat if they could avoid it.

Declan said, "We need to go to dinner."

She smiled. "I am hungry."

"I would be okay if you wanted to slow things down." Not to mention the fact he would be leaving to go back to Washington, DC, soon.

Portia shook her head. "No. I don't need that."

"We'll have a lot of time apart soon. I mean, after we do all the paperwork for the last couple of days."

Portia groaned.

"But while I'm gone we'll have time to talk on the phone, and on video chat. Get to know each other that way. I'll have to put through the paperwork for my resignation."

"Your *what*?"

Declan wanted to smile. "I love you, and you love me. I'm going to resign. Or, I might ask for a transfer. Depends if there's a local office here that needs an agent." He shrugged. "But I'll be back as soon as I can."

"That's it? Just a shrug?"

"Should it be harder than that? I want to be where you are. I want to do life with you."

Portia opened her mouth, then closed it. "I… Maybe not." She paused for a second, all the processing there on her face. "Maybe it shouldn't be harder than that at all. Maybe it should be the simplest thing in the world."

Declan said, "There will be hard times, and rough seasons. But if we stick together then we know we'll always have each other. No matter what job I'm doing, or what case you're working on. At the end of the day, it'll be us."

Portia leaned down and pressed her lips against his. It didn't last nearly long enough to satisfy him, but that day would come. Soon.

"Us," she said.

"Together."

She nodded. "I've been closed off for so long, trying not to feel anything, that now…it's like this has all burst open something inside me. But even still, I feel like if we're together, then everything will be okay."

"I promise it will be."

EPILOGUE

Six months later

Portia drove the lane to her tiny cabin. Waves rolled onto the shore below the hills and cliffs that bordered the coast here. A weather system was moving in, no doubt bringing rain for later. She didn't care much. Not when she'd be by her roaring fire with a hot drink and that throw blanket she loved in about twenty minutes now.

The stress of the last case bled off with every mile she drove. She was ready to curl up and spend some time regrouping. What else could she do when Declan was out of town for work? He'd been gone for two weeks—two of the loneliest of her life.

But that was just this assignment for him, protecting a businessman traveling overseas. He didn't travel much, and she had plenty to keep busy with until got back.

When he did, it would be worth it.

Portia pulled into the drive and frowned. The light in the front window was on—the lamp by her couch.

She parked but didn't collect her duffel from the backseat. Instead, she pulled her weapon and made her way to the front door.

Unlocked.

Inside smelled like sausage and garlic. A familiar smell—her favorite meal. Declan's aunt's spaghetti bake recipe.

"Uh..."

He whirled around, an apron tied at his waist keeping him from getting sauce on his work clothes—pressed pants and a tailored shirt. "You're early! I'm gonna kill Lenny." He slid the pan into the oven and shut the door.

Portia just stared. He had a key since he'd stayed here as well one time when she'd been away in Montana, in the thick of a case, a few weeks ago. When they wanted to spend a few days in La Push together, he got himself a hotel room in town.

He rounded the tiny breakfast bar and crossed the open-plan dining/living room area. Six steps total. "Surprise?"

Portia jumped into his arms. The kiss came fast and made her world shift in its rotation. He held her feet off the floor, those strong arms around her. When she pulled back, Portia touched both sides of his face. "You're back."

"Well, now. If I'd known that was the reaction I'd get to a surprise dinner date..." His voice trailed off and he chuckled.

She grinned back at him. "You made dinner?"

"Don't tell me you stopped for a greasy burger on the way here."

She shook her head.

Declan checked his watch. "It won't be ready for half an hour, and I was going to wait until dessert for this, but you're here...and..."

His head dipped as he settled down on one knee.

Portia stepped back.

"No running." He frowned at her.

"What are you..."

"I'm wrecking this. That's what I'm doing." He wiped his hands on the apron, tugged it off and then stuck a hand in his pants pocket.

He pulled out a tiny velvet box and opened it. "Portia Finch, would you do me the breathtaking honor of being my wife?" He paused for a second. "Preferably as soon as possible."

Portia tore her gaze from the ring and looked at his face. Saw the love there in his eyes.

"Yes. Of course."

He slid the ring on her finger, then swept her up in his arms and spun her around. "I talked to the pastor in town—"

She didn't even need to hear more than that before all the joy in her heart welled up. She laughed. "Of course you did." Why did men always think things were that matter-of-fact? "That makes perfect sense." She shook her head, still laughing.

Declan set her on her feet.

"You moved your whole life out here," she said. "And I know you needed it. I've seen how happy you are with this new job. But I need you to know that I love that you did that, and I appreciate it. So much."

"I know." He kissed her, and she got so caught up in it she almost forgot what she was going to say.

When he lifted his head she said, "The director is retiring."

"We're going to talk about work stuff right now?"

Portia shook her head, smiling. "I'm going to apply for her job."

"You are?"

"I want out of the field. The paperwork and bureaucracy will probably drive me crazy, but I'll have you to keep me sane."

"And…"

He knew there was more. She kissed him once, softly, thankful to God that this man understood her so well. "And the family we can build together." She paused. "Sound good?"

Declan said, "That sounds like the best yes I've ever heard."

* * * * *

If you enjoyed this book,
look for the other books in the
Secret Service Agents series:

Security Detail
Homefront Defenders
Yuletide Suspect
Witness in Hiding
Defense Breach

Dear Reader,

Thank you for joining me on this journey with Portia and Declan. I've wanted to write an NCIS book for a long time and am excited for the possibility of more to come! Portia and Declan are both take-charge people, independent and strong enough to take care of themselves. Sometimes that can seem like a recipe for disaster, but I've found in my own marriage that often it's the similarities between partners that make the relationship stronger.

Portia and Declan both had hurt from the past which scarred them emotionally. Neither was easier or harder to bear than the other—it was simply their experience. Hurts come in all shapes and sizes, but we have a God who delights in being our Comforter. And in bringing people into our lives who will show that comfort to us. I pray that He is doing that for you, and that you can see it.

If you wish to write to me, my email address is lisaphillipsbks@gmail.com and you can find out about my books through www.authorlisaphillips.com.

God bless you richly,
Lisa Phillips

COMING NEXT MONTH FROM

Love Inspired® Suspense

Available April 2, 2019

JUSTICE MISSION

True Blue K-9 Unit • by Lynette Eason

After K-9 unit administrative assistant Sophie Walters spots a suspicious stranger lurking at the K-9 graduation, the man kidnaps her. But she escapes with help from Officer Luke Hathaway. Now, with her boss missing and threats on Sophie's life escalating, can Luke and his K-9 partner save her?

RESCUING HIS SECRET CHILD

True North Heroes • by Maggie K. Black

Trapped with armed hijackers aboard a speeding train in the northern Ontario wilderness, army corporal Nick Henry is determined to free the innocent hostages—especially when he realizes that includes his high school sweetheart, Erica Knight, and the secret son he never knew he had.

IDENTITY: CLASSIFIED

by Liz Shoaf

Someone is convinced security specialist Chloe Spencer has a disc that belongs to him, and he's willing to kill to get it back. But with Sheriff Ethan Hoyt at her side, can she uncover the truth about her past and take down the killer before it's too late?

LETHAL RANSOM

by Laurie Alice Eakes

When Kristen Lang's federal judge mother is kidnapped, the culprits have one ransom demand—her life for her mother's. But Deputy US Marshal Nick Sandoval refuses to let her make the trade. Can he succeed in his mission to keep both Kristen and her mother alive?

UNDERCOVER JEOPARDY

by Kathleen Tailer

Taken hostage in a bank robbery, the last person Detective Daniel Morley expects to find disguised as a robber is his ex-fiancée, FBI agent Bethany Walker. Now, with a mole in law enforcement putting Bethany's life in danger, the only way Daniel can protect her is by joining her undercover.

REUNION ON THE RUN

by Amity Steffen

Framed for her husband's murder and on the run from both the killer and the police, Claire Mitchell needs help if she wants to survive. But when it arrives in the form of her ex-boyfriend, former army ranger Alex Vasquez, can she trust him with her life...and her heart?

LOOK FOR THESE AND OTHER LOVE INSPIRED BOOKS WHEREVER BOOKS ARE SOLD, INCLUDING MOST BOOKSTORES, SUPERMARKETS, DISCOUNT STORES AND DRUGSTORES.

LISCNM0319

SPECIAL EXCERPT FROM

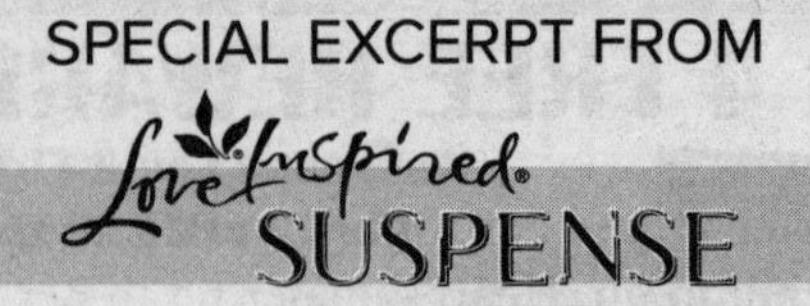

When K-9 administrative assistant Sophie Jordan sees someone tampering with her boss's notes, she finds herself in a killer's crosshairs. Can NYPD K-9 cop Luke Hathaway and his partner keep her safe?

Read on for a sneak preview of Justice Mission *by Lynette Eason, the thrilling start to the True Blue K-9 Unit series, available in April 2019 from Love Inspired Suspense!*

Get away from him.

Goose bumps pebbled Sophie Jordan's arms, and she turned to run. The intruder's left hand shot out and closed around her right biceps as his right hand came up, fingers wrapped around the grip of a gun. Sophie screamed when he placed the barrel of the weapon against her head. "Shut up," he hissed. "Cooperate, and I might let you live."

A gun. He had a gun pointed at her temple.

His grip tightened. "Go."

Go? "Where?"

"Out the side door and to the parking lot. Now."

"Why don't you go, and I'll forget this ever happened?"

"Too late for that. You're coming with me. Now move!"

"You're *kidnapping* me?" She squeezed the words out, trying to breathe through her terror.

LISEXP0319